THE MASQUERADE BALL

The Masquerade Ball

Anita Obehi-Ayemhere

Scribe Tribe™

www.scribetribe.media

THE MASQUERADE BALL

Requests for information should be addressed to:
anitaobehi13@gmail.com or +234 (0) 803 443 2020

Published by:
ScribeTribe Africa
5, Prince Ibrahim Eletu Avenue,
Lekki, Lagos

www.scribetribe.media
hello@scribetribe.media
scribetribeafrica@gmail.com
+234 (0) 708 040 1080, +234 (0) 813 527 3602

Published in Lagos, Nigeria

To my dearly beloved grandfather,
thank you for all the support
and endless trust in
my abilities.

Acknowledgements

The Almighty God: I will forever praise and appreciate the Lord for giving me the wisdom and strength to start and successfully finish my first novel.

My Wonderful Supportive Parents (Dr. Blessing Ayemhere and Mrs. Joy Obehi-Ayemhere): For their countless support throughout this writing period, despite having their daily struggles. I will forever appreciate you both for your immense love and sacrifice that shaped the person that I am today.

My Amazing Siblings (Sophie and Praise): You've both been integral parts of my writing process and I am grateful that I have such wonderful siblings.

My School Administrator, Mrs. Funke Fowler Amba, and School principal, Mrs. Niyatha Krishnan: For giving me a platform that allowed me to challenge and freely express my creative abilities.

My Amazing Teachers: For their encouragement and tolerance throughout my writing journey and pushing me out of my comfort zone, most especially:
- Miss Samuel Amarachukwu
- Miss Evelyn Yakubu
- Aunty Tobi
- Mrs Morenikeji Adebunmi
- Mrs Susan Tayo

My Irreplaceable Classmates/Friends: I sincerely appreciate all of them encouraging me to take this giant risk and finish these first three parts. It hasn't been an easy journey, but because of their support and lively assistance, I could successfully write this book without giving up. I must particularly single out these friends of mine:

- *Oyinkansola Tofade*: The amount of trust, care, support and belief you had in me is what drove me to write in the first place. I am forever grateful I met you 6 years ago and I am so glad I get to acknowledge you in my first book.

- *Hafsoh Busari*: You sacrificed your time to help go through my book, brainstorm title ideas with me and encourage me mentally. Thank you so much for your dedication towards both me and the book!

I also appreciate Bright Ukwenga and the ScribeTribe Africa team for their thorough editing and publishing services to birth this book to reality.

My other supporters include:
- Bisola Olaniboji
- Deborah Nzegwu
- Simisola Cline
- Daniella Akinseli
- Teniola Odiachi
- Esther Kuyebi
- Leila Eneche
- Eniola Agbato
- Olamide Fatunase
- Harriet Ariyo
- Sebasi Bonu

Unfortunately, there are so many people I would love to appreciate that I cannot mention here, but I am sincerely grateful to everyone who cheered me on throughout this journey.

Prologue

The steps got louder.

Instinctively, I shielded myself with my transparent sheets, ordinarily an inconsequential detail but rather unfortunate under these circumstances. My ears pricked up, monitoring the sounds of the nightmare approaching my room. My fingers dug deep into the mattress as I wished I could sink into the foam and disappear. My heart began to pound fiercely out of fear, as if it were desperately trying to escape the cage that limited its freedom. My stomach back flipped repeatedly, and cold sweats broke out on my spine.

My eyes glanced around the room in desperation, hoping to find something–anything–that could protect me, apart from the flimsy sheets I was shrouded in. Nothing. And then the steps halted. I steeled myself, willing my body to relax; but a gulp slid down my throat as I watched them get slowly pushed aside.

The half-lit room revealed the smile on his face. Far from reassuring, instead, it displayed a sinister motive that seeped from his eyes. His fingertips pushed the door lightly, locking it with the key he had successfully stolen from me. A wave of panic rushed through my veins as I shifted backwards, only moving a few inches before the wall behind me halted any hope of actually moving away. He sneered menacingly, making sure that I saw his tongue run over his lips while his eyes scanned my body under the sheets I hid under. I screamed internally, but the sounds got trapped in my throat, and as he locked eyes with me, my heart sank even further.

He approached my bed in short, quick steps, and the oxygen in my lungs froze. My failed effort to merge with the wall led me to give escape another try, and I flung myself off the bed into the farthest direction from his reach. I leaned into the corner of my room and came to the saddening realization that I had nowhere else to run. A mocking laugh rumbled from his throat, and in one swift motion, his strong arms stretched out to capture mine. "Please…" I managed to squeak out, but his eyes only grew darker. "Please…!"

He quickly covered my mouth with his palm, blocking off any attempt to cry for help. His other hand reached into his back pocket, fishing out a once-white handkerchief and forcefully stuffing it between my lips.

"That should keep you quiet," he hissed. The tears that

had welled up in my eyes now spilled over, streaming down in torrents. He smiled again, chillingly, and carried my body back to the bed. As he pinned me down with his hands and knees, he bent close to my ears and whispered, "This won't take long."

Just like that, he raped me effortlessly.

But I wouldn't have guessed that the word 'he' was a mask on its own…

Part One

CHAPTER ONE

It's a Painful Secret

My fork poked around the sausages on my plate, my eyes constantly shifting from my merry parents to the now cold, dejected breakfast.

"You're not eating your food." The sudden question snapped me out of my trance as I slowly lifted my head to meet my mum's eyes.

"Loss of appetite, I replied.

"Please o, don't waste food in my house," she fired back.

My dad shot me a light glare before sipping his milkless tea.

"If you don't finish that food, no dinner for you this evening," His eyes levelled with mine as he carefully placed his personalised mug back on the table. "There are people out there with nothing to eat, and you're here, nonchalantly disregarding a meal that your mates will be grateful to have!"

Almost automatically, the fork stopped being loose in

my palm and became superglued to my fingers. My ears disconnected from the rest of his lecture, my mind wandering far away from the trauma I had been experiencing for the last two months. I could still feel his vice-like grip on my bony arms, the nightmarish smiles that had no bit of sympathy, and his lustful gazes, which inspired nothing but tears.

"Amanda!"

"Sir?" I managed to catch my composure before it flew right past me.

"I said you better not waste that food!"

"Ok, sir!" I sliced the sausages into unequal halves, then reluctantly dumped them in my mouth. What I once considered a satisfying meal had become bland and bitter, and my tongue retracted as another piece of the sausage touched its tip. Contradicting the stinging taste of the sausages, the water, once pure and refreshing, seemed dirty and impure—like how I felt was the current state of my physical and spiritual body. The more bites I took, the stronger my disgust grew for the pancakes and sausages that I had successfully dissected.

An excited "Good morning!" echoed down the stairs, followed by my sister's beaming face. My dad pulled his gaze away from me and directed it at her. "You cannot greet properly?"

Her expression didn't fall or falter as she replied smoothly, "Sorry, daddy. Good morning, daddy. Good morning, mummy.

"You still cannot greet in our language," he said as he shook his head.

"But daddy, you never taught us our language," she quipped back. Her defense was clear and valid: they hadn't once taught us how to speak Beni and had been communicating in English since our childhood.

How were we supposed to have magically acquired the language now that we're older?

My dad didn't respond to her comment and whipped out his phone, indirectly saying he had no reasonable reply and thus ending that part of the conversation. My mum grabbed his empty mug before turning to face Diana again.

"Why did it take you so long to get ready?" I wasn't shocked at my mum's straight-to-the-point questions. She was never one to tip-toe around issues.

She nervously scratched the back of her neck, her eyes roaming around the spacious dining area. My dad, unbothered by her lack of response, exited the table and disappeared up the stairs.

"I spent an hour in the shower...?" Diana started furtively.

A sigh escaped my mum's lips, "How will you eat breakfast then?"

"Well... I'm not hungry, so..."

"You're not going to eat?"

She shrugged with an 'it's just breakfast' expression. My older sister herself wasn't one to be easily flustered.

"Better not let the school call me saying you have a stomach ache," my mum said in resignation.

Diana chuckled lightly before fishing out her tablet from her school bag. Meanwhile, the food I was force-fully shoving down my throat had blatantly refused to digest.

"I feel like throwing up," I muttered, ensuring my mum didn't pick up any of the words I had just said. Throwing up is part of wastage, she once quoted. But my body was rebelling against her statement, and I clasped my hands over my mouth in an attempt to contain the bile racing up my throat.

My eyes landed on my sister, gleefully playing Subway Surfers on her device. She quickly paused the game to grab her headsets and accidentally met my eyes with hers, but she immediately looked away disinterestedly and instantly returned her attention to her school bag, which seemed worth more than my entire existence to her. I felt the liquid slipping through the tiny slits in my teeth. My dad returned in front of us again, his keys rattling loudly. "Time to go!" he called out. In a swift motion, Diana heaved her bags onto her bags and into her arms. You would think she carried books for everyone in the school daily, given the volume she packed to and fro. Meanwhile,

I dashed towards the sink to quickly wash my plates and throw up all the food I had shoved down my throat minutes earlier. The instant satisfaction of an empty stomach was worth the unpleasant mess I left in the sink. I rinsed off the remnants in my mouth and heard my mother cry out from the laundry room, "Who is still in this house?!"

I wasted no time snatching my own bag from the chair, ran out of the door, and waved at the idling car. "I'm here!" I gasped as I jumped into the car, breathless, as if I had just run a marathon. I was no sports enthusiast and did not exercise daily either, so my panting would not have surprised anyone. I looked over at Diana, who now had her headset on, as she blissfully smiled at whatever she was listening to.

Again, she didn't acknowledge my presence - which by now I was used to and shouldn't have bothered me, but it did still.

Maybe it was because this was how our sisterly relationship was from the very moment I was born. She had mostly ignored me since we were children, and I never knew why. My earliest memory of her as an older sister was of Diana snapping at me for playing with her toys, and even now, the only way she communicates with me is either in attack mode or when she needs me to do something.

Or maybe it was because I had something more

significant to be bothered about, something that could cause her entire life to shatter just by hearing about it.

With the kind of predicament I found myself trapped in, my family should have been the first people I confided in, but my mum would probably either faint or pray about my lack of virginity for the rest of my life. My dad would be upset, but only until he was distracted by the next business meeting. My sister would present my case as a sob story to all her friends in school.

Those were most likely assumptions of how they might react, but then again, there was no direct, calm, or constructive way of saying, 'I'm being raped every night in our house!' without raising any suspicions about my own possible culpability.

'Who gets raped every night and doesn't scream at least once?'

Well, me.

Why? Because I am unable to cry out when it happens and choose not to burden others by informing them about my sudden lack of virginity, especially with how it happened.. I would rather bear all the pain myself than become everyone's pity case whenever they see me. Besides, even if I eventually did tell my parents, they would find some twisted way to make it my fault for being his target in the first place.

"Maybe it was your dressing or the way you carried yourself. I'm sure you were involved with boys somehow in school before; that's why it's your fault— "

My mother's voice broke my reprieve. "See this child! You forgot your water bottle!" Just the woman I was thinking about. Her booming tone instantly dusted my imaginative clouds away and replaced them with headaches.

"Then you'd get to school and start saying you're thirsty." I sighed, respectfully taking the bottle from her hands.

I could hear a light hiss from the passenger on my right side, but my ears ignored it.

"Alright then, have a good day!" Mummy called out before finally entering the house.

I didn't dare close my eyes to think as my dad reversed out of the gates because the darkness and nighttime were closely related to each other, if not practically twins. And my nights were already real-life nightmares.

CHAPTER TWO

Things Have Changed

"Goodbye daddy, love you!" He merely nodded as my sister flew out of the car. I was shocked at how she could race away with three rock-weight bags strapped to her body. She didn't seem to mind, as the superhuman that she often was, and she proceeded to wave excitedly at one of her best friends, who arrived at the same time as we did.

I grudgingly got out of the car; my reaction was the complete opposite of Diana's. Unlike her, carrying my backpack felt like carrying the air, yet my movement made it seem like I was propping against a tree to prevent it from falling over. Eventually, my whole body made it out of the car, my feet clumsily turning towards the bright, welcoming school.

"So, you can't say thank you?" My dad snapped from inside the car. "Do you think it's convenient for me to drive you to school every day, like I don't have work to do? Thank you, daddy." No reply. Instead, he put the car in reverse, signifying the end of our non-conversation. I hung my head low as I walked through the glass doors into school.

This place used to make me smile, but the only thing I'd felt for the past two months was dreadful numbness, random panic attacks, and uncontrollable tears. I had transformed from a regular secondary school girl into what must be the worldwide winner of the babies' crying competition. The number of times my emotions displayed themselves without warning in a day should be equivalent to the number of times I blinked in an hour, resulting in countless phone calls from the school authorities to my parents to discuss the emotional well-being of their daughter, leading to my mum praying for the next four days and my dad... my dad wasn't even mentally present for the meetings.

I wandered like a lost penguin until I finally spotted my classroom sign on the newly painted walls. As I stepped into the empty classroom, I remembered how I used to be one of the students who rushed into the class at the last minute.

We were never actually late to school, but we all enjoyed chatting and roaming the place before it was time for attendance. We'd throw ourselves into the classroom, laughing as our class teacher—utterly unperturbed by the presence of his students flat on the concrete surface, would stride in and take attendance in a monotonous voice.

These days, I'm the first student to occupy the classroom, as there's nowhere to go when you're not having fun and living freely. The desperation in my heart to turn back time and warn my two-month-old self to lock her doors that night—despite the strict tones of my mother specifically warning me against doing so—still screamed from my insides.

For once, breaking the rules would've led to a much brighter future for me than being molested daily and being lily-livered to report the disgusting perpetrator.
My isolated corner, drowned in heavy, dark energy, pulled me over. I set my weightless bag down and dragged my table a few inches away from the desks before me. I heard my chair scraping against the wall behind me, letting me know that the distance between me and everyone else was perfect. It was better that my breakdowns in class didn't disturb the untainted aura of the other students I hid behind.

"Finally, peace," I said to myself. But that was a lie. This wasn't a peaceful reflection moment for me; it was another opportunity to remind myself that my life had been flipped over in a matter of hours.

I didn't have much time to reflect because two other students engaged in a pointless argument interrupted my sulking. Thankfully, I remained unnoticed as they carried on.

"You are mad. Snickers chocolate is the best!"

"No! It's Kit-Kat."

"Snickers has way more contents than just milk and Choco dust."

"And Kit-Kat is crunchy, unlike that draggy chocolate bar."

I watched Olivia roll her eyes at Chima, who ignored her reaction and sprinted towards his desk for whatever reason. She flung her school bag onto her preferred chair, located in the row I now hated with all my heart.

The front row.

"I wonder who willingly sits where everyone can see you."

Flashback

"Amanda, where would you like to sit?" Cynthia asked as we stepped into our new classroom.

"The front row, duh!" I replied instantly, "That's the fastest seat out of the class! And short break time is like a war zone."

She tapped her chin briefly, then nodded, "It's true o. That place is usually hectic. Being the first in line is always good."

"And gets us the hot snacks! The freshest ones—the ones they make and bring out like that."

"Abi ooo." She dragged out the chair next to the one I had excitedly claimed, "Abeg, let me sit beside you; your head is working well."

Present Day

Oh, right, that's where I also used to sit with my ex-friend Cynthia. We were always so happy to enter an empty snack hall and be the first students to purchase the allotted snacks for that day. Good times.

"So much has changed, huh?"

I shook my head in disappointment, then snapped out of my daze and started watching Olivia again. She had begun doing back stretches by her table. I blankly watched her little exercise, zoning out into my dark space ten seconds after watching her. My mind spun me back into that dark reality; the pain from last night was resurfacing, causing my face and stomach to twist in agony.

"Olivia ooo, you better not break your back with all your unusual stretches."

My watery eyes snapped open, and I swiftly turned to stare at Danielle, casually leaning against the doorframe.

Her eyes remained fixed on Olivia, and she began slowly shaking her head.

"See this one o. Who are you shaking your head for?" Olivia shot back.

"You, of course." She quickly waved at Chima, struggling to plug his headphones in, then focused on Olivia again.

"Exercise at home, not in your school uniform."

Olivia scoffed out loud, "Who are you, my mother?"

"I forbid such a thing."

Olivia's mouth dropped, "So you're saying it's bad to be my mother."

"No o!" She retorted, "I'm saying your mother is trying o. To handle such a human being, me, I could never."

My ears ached while listening to the bickering between two teenage girls over a senseless topic. Still, my mind told me it was better to endure their argument than return to my haunted nightmare for reality. Anything that could extract and distract me from that 'beautiful place' was worth it.

"And you look like a frog!" Danielle threw a victory pose, mocking Olivia's inability to shoot a smooth comeback. Another lovely eye roll was given to her, but Danielle laughed it off.

"Abeg, can you guys, like, quiet down? I want to listen

to Asake." Then he suddenly spun his head around and caught my eyes.

Oh no.

"Chai, see this girl o, she's really become emo. I did not even notice her there."

My undisturbed corner had been broken through, almost like destroying a fourth wall.

Both girls also spun around to stare at me, then gaped and dropped their jaws at me. Next, they skipped towards my cemetery in a corner.

Well, Olivia skipped while Danielle casually walked over.

"Where have you beeeen?" Olivia squealed; her arms tightly locked around my neck.

"Right here this entire time," I replied weakly.

It had completely slipped my mind that the three students who had each claimed a portion of our spaceless classroom were my three friends. Correction: The friends who remained attached to me after my so-called emo phase began. The rest said I was ruining their happy vibes with my contrasting gloomy spirit.

Not that they were wrong, though.

"Girl, how long does this phase usually last?" Olivia questioned, but I just shrugged.

I'm not going through an emo phase; I'm trapped in a nightmare loop.

"Probably a couple of months," Danielle replied in an intellectual tone.

"Well, the phase should pass quickly so she can turn normal again!"

"Or enter a girly phase where she experiments with make-up and dresses." Danielle facepalmed at Olivia's comment while Chima jumped out of his chair.

"We're still here for you, Mandy, even if you become a psychopath."

I already feel like one.

"Yeah! For once, he makes sense!"

"What do you mean for once?!" He stomped over and hovered over Olivia's bossy status, "I always make sense!"

"Not at all."

"Sometimes I even wonder how you got into SS2 when you have the thinking capacity of a rat." He let out a bear's growl, and they all continued tossing insults above my head while I started admiring my watch to distract myself.

Honestly, their noise wasn't bothering me; it was a blessing from God to keep my mind out of the unfortunate situation I had fallen into. Deep down, I was extremely grateful I still had friends who chose to stick by me during what they thought was a spell of adolescent angst. I'd considered spilling the mortifying truth to them countless times, but the idea of burdening friends who already had their issues kept my lips sealed.

"Amanda, this boy is very annoying." She pouted as Chima snorted in amusement.

I stared blankly at her until she did her iconic eye roll while Danielle returned to her desk.

"Danieeeeeeeeelle!"

"Don't drag me into this." Olivia skipped towards her table, completely ignoring her request not to do precisely what she was about to do. Chima lightly patted my back before returning to his desk, and I slumped into my seat.

Less than a few minutes after the morning bickering among my friends ended, other cliques of students began emerging through the doorway in groups of threes and fives. Apparently, every classmate of mine had at least two friends.

Myself not excluded.

Some people thankfully didn't pay attention to me, but some oversabi girls shot strange looks at me, eyeing my clothes from top to bottom.

"Look, the crybaby is wearing another dead outfit," I heard one say in a high-pitched voice, sounding like something from an anime movie.

Her dedication to being a mean girl must have caused her to forget that we were in a private school where we all had to wear similar uniforms, to break all sorts of barriers between the rich and the poor, or the privileged and less privileged. Her snide remark couldn't make a dent on me, and even if it wanted to, my whole body had already been hit with something much worse than a measly insult.

I was a girl swimming in an ocean of trauma; these frivolous barbs weren't the reason for my tears anymore. I shook my head and found myself saying, "People are just—"

"—so stupid!" Someone else yelled out.

Great! My sentence was completed for me. Now, it won't bug me that I insulted a fellow human being the way my mum warned us not to ever do, because I never finished the statement.

Simi, the girl who had just finished my sentence, was screaming her lungs out at Joshua, her on-and-off boyfriend. Her friends were not even trying to hold her back. Instead, they were shouting along with her in their clash of shrill and gruff voices. He then foolishly proceeded to aggravate the argument by flinging his headphones on right in front of her. Her palm cracked across his face in a thunderous slap. The class chorused 'Haaaa!' as the slap echoed around each corner of the room. Nothing could ever beat the daily dose of early morning drama.

"All of you at that table right now, Similoluwa and Co, to Mr. Okoko's office. Now!"

Mr. Adebayo, our class teacher and supervisor, pointed towards the door and waited for them to swallow down their pride and leave his classroom. I could hear Simi's proud hiss before shuffling past Joshua.

"Joshua, so you came from your class to cause trouble in my class!"

"I'm sorry, sir," Joshua said, still wincing at the slap.

"Foolish boy," Simi spat. The class snorted at her comment while Mr. Adebayo stomped his feet and impatiently pursued them out of his class.

Afterwards, he took attendance. His intimidating stance dared students to make noise.

"Folakemi."

"Present Sir!"

"Olivia."

"I'm here, Sir."

"Just say present like a normal human being." Bola, the class clown, muttered loud enough for the entire class to hear. The class erupted in silent giggles as Olivia spun around in her chair and eyeballed him until he withered in his seat before turning back to face forward. "Are you all done with your side talks and laughs, or should I allow someone else to take my place up here?" The class fell silent again, a perfect answer to his indirect question.

"Grace."

"Present Sir!"

The roll call continued, but one of the dangers of the mind is its ability to wander off into your happiest or darkest memories, regardless of how noisy or quiet your environment is. In a larger class, it would probably take the teacher a while to reach my name in the well-worn register, but as soon as my head landed on my freezing desk, I was plunged into my unsettling memories.

Flashback

"I just want a small taste of you, baby," he whispered rabidly.

"Please, sir… please!" He grabbed my wrists tightly, roughly pinning them against the wall. His eyes were hungry as he hitched up my nightdress.

"Please—"

He smirked and forced his lips on mine while I wept. Seconds later, he pulled back and successfully slipped off the night dress.

"You're going to enjoy this, I promise you."

"No…" His large hand trapped my whole mouth, his other hand unzipping his trousers as swiftly as he could. I closed my eyes in fear, my skin reacting to his hot breath beside my neck.

"Finally…"

And with that, he…

Present Day

"—Amanda Ekhator!"

"She's present, sir!" That sounded like Olivia.

My body visibly shook as I raised my head off my wooden desk. It was soaked with tears.

I dug my hands into my backpack, thankful I had a little tissue roll stuffed at the bottom.

"Amanda!"

I continued rubbing the tissue over my eyes, but I knew the redness would still be visible.

"Toilet… pressed… sorry sir!"

"Ama—" I was already out the door, heading towards the toilet as fast as my legs could move. After running the wrong way three times and accidentally bumping into a couple making out behind the stairway doors, I finally threw myself into the female bathroom, collapsing on the floor immediately.

"Urgh…" I didn't know how long I stayed there before stumbling up from the ground, my eyes streaked with tears. I splashed water all over my face until I was calm enough to make a sentence without shaking.

"I... am... fine..." I repeated the lies to myself as I stared at my reflection. The torn, broken, and frightened part of me was all I could see, causing my head to spin and my vision to blur again.

"Why... why did it have to be me?" I aggressively splashed water at my distorted image, panting hard as more tears began to flow. I was incredibly grateful that no one had followed me into the restroom out of care or concern.

My heavy breakdown wasn't something I wanted others to witness.

CHAPTER THREE

I Can't Focus

"And that's how you solve the equation of a line. Any question?" Mrs. Damilola asked with a soft smile, but my expression didn't reciprocate her softness. Fortunately, she didn't look in my direction and couldn't see my spiritless corner.

"It seems we all understand the formula," she continued. I didn't, but I wasn't willing to learn it either.

After lightly struggling with uncapping the marker, she wrote practice questions on the whiteboard.

A collective groan soared around the classroom.

"Mrs. Damilola, class is almost over." Bola pointed out smugly.

She gracefully turned around to face her bold challenger and said, "We have about ten minutes left, Bola." Her soft tone didn't change.

"Ma, that won't be enough to solve those equations."

"I agree, ma! It's too much."

One after the other, each student began defending

one another and their right to enjoy the remaining ten minutes before the 'terror class', aka Biology, came up next.

I didn't join in their protests, mostly because I had been mentally unavailable throughout the last five periods:

◆ Civic Education to Economics with teachers who had the voices of megaphones but the audibility of mice.

◆ Double period of Accounting—with the insistent teacher who always reported my absence to the principal, and then shooting me frustrated looks when she realised that I was yet to be punished with something more severe than toilet cleaning.

◆ English Literature with Romeo and Juliet being the only story from all her classes that my brain chose to remember. Oddly enough, I didn't even take her classes, so she paid more attention to her core students and their terrible interpretation skills, rather than my lifeless attitude during her period.

I had spent those five periods deeply analysing the depth of my depressive reality. It gave me more time to think widely and observe all the little details of my life I had never appreciated before—like passing silly notes during class or commenting on every wrong English some teachers used to lighten up the depressing class atmosphere.

Now, I had turned into that depressing class atmosphere.

"Pages 225 to 227." My attention turned back to class; my ears pricked up as I tried to catch onto the ongoing lesson.

"Thank you, ma!" That meant their conversation was over, and I had missed out on vital information needed to boost the points of my continuous assessment.

But did I care? Not one bit.

The unfortunate bell rang, and a mix of 'Noooo's! and 'Urghhhh's! filled the air. I had spent six periods of the whole day crying and hating my life, and the plan for the remaining four periods required no physical labour or mental stress.

All I planned to do was attempt to sleep because I certainly couldn't sleep at night anymore.

"Amanda ooo! Please, do you have your WAEC biology textbook? I think I forgot mine at home."

I reluctantly lifted my head from my desk, "But you're a boarder."

She nodded, answering the rest of my unspoken questions. I rested my head on my desk again while dipping my hand underneath my table, hoping to hit a thick booklet I'd assumed would be the textbook.

A few seconds passed before I finally looked back at her, "Nope, didn't bring it."

"Of course, you didn't," she said curtly.

Yes, judge me for not bringing my textbook as a day student when you didn't get yours as a boarder. I can bring mine tomorrow, while you must wait another month!

I was shouting those words at her and smirking, all in my head. The energy to open my mouth and scream those words at her was already consumed by my emotional distress. But this torturous cycle has gone on for more than two months now, and I sadly got used to this lifestyle after a while.

I couldn't allow myself be hysterical throughout the day. I would rather break down for some part of the day and stay numb for the rest of it.

"I'm shocked that man is late to class." Danielle had somehow gotten beside me, her body taking its usual form of leaning against the wall.

"Never thought I'd witness the day," I mumbled in response to her statement.

We both went silent for a while, my eyes observing the weird posters on the wall with the heading 'NEVER GIVE UP' coloured like the rainbow.

"I wish…" She broke the silence between us, ignoring

the background noise of the TikTokers in our classroom.

"Hmm...?"

"I wish that I could just... breathe," my mind quickly flashed the words 'Incoming Rant', warning me not to say anything stupid.

"It's tiring studying for hours, yet I never feel satisfied with any of my efforts. Even if I got 100 per cent in everything, they'd still find something to shame me for. And I don't know if this is supposed to be normal, but I'm honestly stressed." I looked at Danielle, trying to form the appropriate words to say to her, as we both looked at the movement by the door.

Mr. Aloba's laptop peeped into our classroom, closely followed by a junior student who gingerly held it away from his body, then by Mr. Aloba himself, holding a human skeleton in his right hand.

"Well, time for Bio. At least you're free this period," she sighed. That's even true. Thank God I dropped it!

Danielle quickly rubbed my back and returned to her desk, giving me no time to comment, respond, or comfort her. Well, I wouldn't have known whether to say 'sorry', 'good luck,' or 'things will get better', but at least she could share her pain with me.

Meanwhile, I still hadn't found the keys to my voice.

"Good afternoon, class. Sorry, I am late." The drawn-out 'Good afternoons' he got in response made it clear that we would have preferred if he never came to class at all. I wasn't wishing him bad luck in whatever he did outside of teaching us about the millions of cells in our system (that no one asked to know about), but Biology was just this bulky subject that didn't seem to have an end. It was like writing a sentence without a full stop, indicating there's still a lot more to say.

"Today, we'll be learning about the skeletal system!" His enthusiasm hadn't landed on anyone in class, but that didn't dampen his zest. After connecting his computer to our class TV, he picked up the human skeleton he had brought to class and held it up in the air.

"Now this," he started, grabbing the attention of only a few students, "is a human skeleton. Please pass it around the class."

I knew it would never reach me unless someone turned around and sighted my corner. I had no interest in his lesson, but my eyes found interest in the skeleton they passed around. It looked familiar, like a human being I had once known before they passed away. The more I stared at it, the more precise the shape became in my head.

Only if he was dead too.

The skeleton also looked a lot like my unwanted night visitor, and I prayed to God that he was actually dead and my nights wouldn't contain real nightmares anymore.

But one can only wish.

"Excuse me, sir, but did you murder someone to get this skeleton?" Bola asked with fake concern and the class erupted in spontaneous laughter.

"No, I did not kill anyone. This is a preserved human skull that I repurchased some months ago," Mr Aloba replied, as he adjusted his tie nervously.

That was a little suspicious, I thought to myself.

"Sure, you 'bought' it?" Bola persisted. Everyone laughed until Mr. Aloba banged the table with his palm in annoyance. He seemed agitated and shaken up. It was weird that such a banal joke could bother a teacher's stance that much.

Unless… it wasn't a joke.

And if it wasn't, I will start praying now that he somehow discovered my secret, hunted down the man, and subtly murdered him. But if it isn't who I hope it is, then wow!

Such dedication to acquire a skull to teach his class! Go him!

"Quiet everyone, or else you'll all be reported to the principal."

My gaze on him remained unbroken as I watched him finally regain his composure and halt all the nervous sweat that threatened to start streaming down his head. Afterwards, he searched for a video on his laptop for us to watch and 'enjoy'. With little interest, I flipped my face over on my desk and stared intently at the wall beside me. The little cracks between them indicated how old it was, and it didn't surprise me that the school only took care to repaint the walls which were mainly visible to visitors. A soft "Oh well!" escaped my lips as my body relaxed to enter a sleeping position—if I could sleep.

The noise from my classmates slowly fizzled away, and I entered a new world I was forcing my mind to think about. I knew how easy it was to slip into those nightmares, but for once, I needed to find something positive about how my life currently was.

Sadly, nothing was positive except my relationship with my friends. And even that wasn't enough to sustain the remaining periods I had today.

CHAPTER FOUR

It Tastes Different

"I've been hungry all day." Olivia groaned before hurriedly shoving a massive spoonful into her mouth.

"You ate during short break na."

"I swear. Is it not you who bought three doughnuts and still took three people's sausages?" Danielle inquired.

"Ehnnn, they did not want it na. Plus, I did not eat breakfast."

"Tah! That's a lie. You bragged about how tall your pancake stack was this morning."

"Food is food jor." There were hisses around the table as Olivia shrugged, taking another massive bite of her food.

"This food is so nice! Abeg Amanda, collect food for me if you're not eating."

I only had to stare at her for a few seconds before she exhaled defeatedly.

Today was Tuesday—the happiest lunch day for the entire school, including the teachers, admin, and cleaning staff. The lunch ladies prepared Nigeria's most cherished one-of-a-kind meal. The meal causes mouths to water, eyes to pop, noses to dance, and stomachs to rumble. The meal that a foreigner's tongue will touch and cause them to spiral into a world of enjoyment with the spices decorating your mouth with beautiful flavours and the bright orange colour attracting all creatures on land, air and even the sea. The meal that could solve world hunger by eating just a grain of its body: jollof rice.

"This jollof is sweet o," Chima remarked with a massive smile.

Not just jollof rice, the party version of the jollof rice. The type prepared at parties in bulk that could fill more than twenty bathtubs with plenty leftovers.

Students kept staring intently at me as they shoved rice down their throats. Being the only student in the school to skip the most awaited lunch day every week made me uncomfortable. And while this seemingly gratifying meal made everyone's school day a thousand times better, the only thing I smelt was a heated combination of various spices; the orange flavour caused my stomach to churn, and if I took even one bite, I'd have a repeat of the first Tuesday I experienced after the molestation started.

Flashback

"Hey, Mandy!" Someone shouted from across the hallway as I painfully exited the restroom. I instinctively jumped back in fear before it registered that it was just Chima.

"Yeah…?" I choked out. The amount of vomit I had let out didn't seem to be enough, as my body radiated continuous pain that constantly hit my stomach. I felt like collapsing, but Chima was already by my side.

"You good? You acted like you had seen a ghost." Concern dripped from his voice, but I couldn't even nod. Throughout the day, his face seemed to be plastered on every person and thing I walked by; constantly watching my back and front, no matter where I resided, was becoming extremely stressful.

He whistled to Danielle, Olivia, and Cynthia, who were heading to lunch. Upon seeing my state, they swiftly spun around, and Olivia was the first person to rush towards me.

"Girl, are you sure you're okay?"

"I… I feel sick." I held my head in both of my hands in an attempt to steady my brain and my mind.

Danielle quickly touched my forehead, "You feel warm. Let's go to the nurse."

"She's already gone." Cynthia chimed in, "Took her even before classes started. She fainted right in the middle of attendance."

Because I thought I saw the man's face on every student, including females. He was haunting me, even during the day.

"Hmmm...," Olivia tapped her chin thoughtfully, trying to brainstorm a new solution.

"Well, today's Tuesday." She stated. All eyes—even mine which were weak and blurry—fell on her.

"And...?"

"It's Jollof Rice. Let her eat at least five spoons of rice to have something in her system."

Danielle and Cynthia quickly shook their heads, "She's throwing up, and you want her to try and eat?"

"Um, duh?"

"No way."

"Come on, guys, even if she ate breakfast, she'd have thrown it all up by now." Olivia nodded at Chima's defence of her.

"Finally, I agree with you for once." He just chuckled lightly before gesturing to Danielle to take my other arm. Then, they slowly dragged my almost-collapsing body to the lunch hall, which had already taken up the whole school.

The smell everyone was trying to savour made me feel somewhat nauseous. The lovely scent of freshly cooked rice was replaced with an odour that my nose couldn't accurately detect. The floor tiles seemed to wobble and looked unbalanced; the ceiling was falling in slow motion; and even the students all walked like drunkards carrying massive plates of rice and chicken.

My body fell backwards as the man's face reflected off the euphoric students, and my eyes widened in horror.

"Amanda, what's going on?" Danielle's voice tickled my ears, but my heart tried to steady itself from the frightening shock. Chima signalled to Folakemi, Joshua and Naomi, all seated at our usual table. They managed to set me down on the chair without my body tipping over, as Olivia waved at us from the lunch line, receiving odd yet nonchalant stares as she boldly held two plates.

"What's wrong with Mandy?" Joshua questioned before taking a quick sip from his bottle.

My head closed the gap between itself and the lunch table, my fingers blocking all smells from entering my nose. I sighted Naomi's eyes as she peeked at my pitiful state before withdrawing back into her chair.

"Nurse's office?"

"Been there." Tears began to brim in my eyes, but this was the wrong time to be a cry-baby.

Olivia's squeal grew closer, letting us know she had successfully acquired the two meals from the line.

"This is for you." The steam slightly messed with my eyesight; my body temperature rose just by being so close to the meal. I felt a heated pair of hands push my drowsy head off the table, a genuine smile greeting me as I sat upright.

"Why are you treating her like a baby?" A nosy teacher queried, scanning me from top to bottom. Folakemi cleared her throat before respectfully replying.

"She's sick, sir."

"And she couldn't stay in the nurse's office?"

"No, sir."

"Is she willing to eat?"

"Yes, sir."

He looked unsatisfied with the answers but retired from our table and went on to bother another set of chattering students. My eyes glared down at the meal before me; my stomach lurching upwards, warning me not to eat the rice.

The persistence of my friends was more compelling. "Please eat na, just a bite." Cynthia, already halfway down with her meal, began dragging my untouched plate towards her side. I flinched at the sound of Naomi's hand slapping hers away.

"Is it your food?" She grumbled silently and shoved another spoonful into her mouth. Joshua continuously took sips of his water bottle, but his eyes stayed on me throughout his water sessions.

"I'm really not hungry…"

"Just a bite! One bite is fine if you can't eat the rest!"

"If she doesn't want to eat it, please pass her plate." She received another arm slap from Naomi.

"Amanda..." The concern in Danielle's voice kept rising, and the guilt started to poke me. With my remaining strength, I held my breath and took a mini bite of my now lukewarm lunch.

"10 minutes left! Eat fast!"

"See? It wasn't so bad!" Olivia beamed as she finally sat and devoured her chicken like a starving beast. While the five of them watched her compulsively eat away, my body visibly rejected the bite I had taken.

"Guys..."

"Olivia, why do you eat like you've never seen food in your life?"

"Guys... please..."

"See this one o! When you are faced with deliciousness, you give it your all."

"Ode."

"Guy—" A displeasing and horrifyingly dull rainbow shot out of my throat, leaving a burning sensation in the middle of my oesophagus. The stench destroyed my nostrils and sent carbon dioxide back into my lungs as the air couldn't successfully mix with anything. My friends leapt away from the table, except for Cynthia. She unfortunately then got sprayed with all of my undigested swill.

My eyes pleaded with her while the retch from my mouth continued to hose her down, expectedly shattering her self-esteem in the process. I slumped onto the ground as the world resumed its spinning cycle, the man's creepy smirk rotating around my head as I passed out.

Present Day

I remembered what made Cynthia cut ties with me now: it was after drenching her in vomit, causing her extreme embarrassment, and making her the talk of school for many months.

"And the spaghetti yesterday was too soggy. Amanda, are you even here?" My consciousness woke up to Olivia's fingers snapping around my face.

"Yes, I'm here." At least I am now.
Chima's face fell onto the table, his eyes morphing into puppy eyes as he addressed me.

"Can I pweaseeeeee have your wice?"

"Ew!" He rubbed his head in agony while Danielle cracked her knuckles after she had just slammed his head onto the table.

"Why did you beg with the voice of a three-year-old child?"

He rearranged his facial expression and shrugged, unfazed by his abnormal display of desperation. I wanted to laugh and comment on his dramatic behaviour, but the burdensome weight that pressed down my throat and mind reminded me that times had changed, and so had my life, leading me to stare blankly while my three companions exchanged jokes throughout the forty-minute break.

As it appeared as though the only task my eyes now had was mindlessly looking about, I examined the lunch hall wordlessly. The young, vibrant juniors at the starting line were engaged in harmless fun; the older, mature seniors were having appropriate and inappropriate discussions over a hot meal (girls about boys, and boys about girls); the staff were exchanging boasts about their favourite students, and even the lunch ladies were laughing and joking in their native languages. A pretty normal lunch break by all estimation.

My gaze was about to return to my amusing friends when the sight of a teardrop halted my eyes. The girl, with her braids neatly tied in a stable bun, had her back facing me, but her cheeks were still clearly visible, and so was the teardrop I had seen slide down that very cheek. Curiosity rocked my brain speedily, my eyes still glued to the mysterious junior.

"Amanda! Chima said the chicken thigh is tastier than the drumstick!" I turned around to face the two teenage babies arguing, while Danielle's expression reflected her genuine tiredness of their endless bickering.

I sighed slightly, "Difference in tastes, I guess."

"Difference in tastes ke? They all taste the same!"
"Yes, but the drumstick is way juicier than the thigh!"
And here we go again…

CHAPTER FIVE

Numb Artistic Drive

The English teacher's microphone voice announced that our break was officially over. A rush of loud shuffling, colliding plates, and chatter rose to the maximum volume level as mobs of students flew out the door. My eyes caught a brief glimpse of the droplet girl's face. I concluded that the scar on her right eye was from a recent incident. And still, the burning curiosity inside me was eager to dig deeper.

"Ohhh, we have Geographyyyy", Olivia stated.

"You have Geography; I have Technical Drawing."

Olivia shot pitiful daggers at Danielle as they dropped their oily plates, which had pieces of chicken bone sliding across them.

"Must suck to draw all those weird line construction thingies."

"Must suck to draw the entire map of Nigeria with a compass and broomstick." She lightly shoved Danielle aside and playful stomped a short distance away from her while Chima tried engaging me in small talk.

"What class do you have again?"

I answered dryly, "Visual Art. Don't you already know this?"

"I do." He mindlessly kicked a rock as we approached the towering flights of stairs. "I was just wondering how you were going to create anything when you're in such a," he paused for a second, "moody phase."

I didn't feel the need to defend or comment on his statement, so we walked side-by-side in an unsettling silence. The most straightforward answer would've been: 'Well, I suffer every night, so I can't exactly be creative when I have an uninvited visitor in my room every night who seems to hold a lot of sexual desires and chose to explore them with a teenage girl instead of his wife.'

But I obviously cannot say that.

Exactly five minutes after ascending the stairs, he turned to face me again. "Take care of yourself."

With that, he turned on his heel and headed towards Technical Drawing, frantically waving at Danielle and Jeremiah before they disappeared down the stairs again.

I dragged my feet towards the Arts lab with heavy, lethargic steps. On my way, I sighted the geography students in the adjacent classroom, laughing at their black-and-white video projection. At the same time, their cantankerous teacher, Mr. Godwin, sat in the teacher's corner, no doubt regretting his decision to become a teacher.

Eventually, I arrived beside the door that refused to identify as one plain, simple colour instead of the checkered slab of wood it had become.

"Amanda, you cannot just stand outside when the class is taking place indoors."

Somehow, Mr. Benjamin caught a glimpse of me from his peripheral, unapproving deep voice hypnotising my feet, and ferrying them inside the classroom in spite of my reluctance to actually enter. I credit him for being the first teacher to actually pay attention to me throughout the day.

I observed the other three students here with me: two classmates and a science student from our neighbouring class. I grabbed my drawing pad from the top of his artistic desk before settling down on the donkey bench, directly opposite the other artists.

"Today's lesson is carving." He started to write his name on the whiteboard, which wasn't necessary to me but must be his way of helping students with short-term memory to remember his full name—until the marker faded mid-way.

Mr. Benjamin Akpola.

And yes, we call him by his first name in an African school environment, unlike all his other colleagues.

Fire him and expel us.

"My marker has finished," he said quietly, as though he were the student and we, the teacher.

"Sir, I have a spare marker in my pencil case!" Fisayo yelled and fished out his marker which he stole three weeks ago before handing it over to Mr. Benjamin in an exaggerated fashion as if he just solved World Hunger and was receiving a trophy for it.

Mr. Benjamin smiled in appreciation and approached the board again to complete his name. Afterwards, he tossed the marker on his desk and continued his lesson.

"Just like everything else, carving also has its definition." He gestured towards our notepads, which everyone quickly opened except for me. I generally had little to no interest in all the lessons, but the fact that he acknowledged my existence meant that I could give him a quarter of my attention in return. The rest of my attention was glued to his head, perfectly reflecting some light off the ceiling. His hands resembled those of a nursery student who was handed paint without supervision.

"Now carving is the reduction of mass of an object," he started dramatically, "to create! A shape, or An object."

"So basically, destroying an object to make an object out of the destroyed object," Ayomide pointed out. What she said clicked perfectly in my brain.

He paused to stare at her momentarily stunned before clearing his throat, "No, it is not that."

"But that's what you said."

"No, I said it was the reduction of mass."

"Sir!" He groaned as Ayomide wiggled her arm in the air in a confused state.

"Dayo's the only science student in this class, but you're speaking in Physics language."

"It's just basic English." Dayo clicked his tongue in annoyance, causing Ayomide's frustration to skyrocket. Meanwhile, Fisayo was scribbling away on his drawing pad, waiting for the class to continue appropriately.

"That's enough, everyone. Moving on." The distinct smell of soap diffused around the room, leaving a sweet yet pestering smell in my nostrils.

"Now, this is a bar of soap." He didn't need to point that out.

The rest of the class stared at the soap bar like a diamond treasure. My attention was diverted slightly, but I returned to the class to honour the teacher's outstanding memory.

"We can carve this soap bar using various tools, like a chisel, or even files!"

"Files as in documents?"

"No, ode." Fisayo facepalmed in annoyance, "Files as in, files!"

"Yeah, that explanation makes so much sense."

"Everyone, please keep quiet and pay attention!"

"Nope, Mr. Benjamin Akpola," I said in my head. "That's the maximum amount of attention I can invest in your period."

A glance at my watch told me it was almost 3:20 p.m., but they continued their argument since the teacher wasn't in strict control of his classroom environment, despite having only four students.

As my eyes landed on the windows connected to the corridors, I spotted Mr. Adebayo and Miss. Funmilayo exit the staff lounge with worrisome expressions plastered all over their faces. They quickly split into opposite directions, and I ducked underneath the window to avoid being spotted. My mind pondered what could have occurred within the staff lounge.

It raised my curiosity to its maximum level.

"What is this one doing?" Dayo singled me out; curiously looking at me crouched beneath the window frame.

The bell screamed loudly for a couple of seconds before dying down. I glared at Dayo and wished I could smirk back at his taunting question.

"Buy your bars of soap before our next class!" Mr. Benjamin shouted as I bounced out of the art room, switching to a sluggish pace when I neared my classroom. Thankfully, everyone had split up into their desired—or forced—subjects, so I didn't have to deal with the crew as I retrieved my bag.

"Of course, you're leaving early." I grabbed my pen quickly as it tumbled down my desk before responding to Danielle.

"Well, I'm not going home but leaving the classroom, so yeah." I wasn't rushing because I was excited to return to my house, nor was I eager to spend my remaining mentally stable time in my depressing corner of the building with dusty, cramped stacks of outdated books they labelled a library.

"I see." She shot me a bittersweet smile containing a lot of messages I couldn't clearly dissect yet. She also proceeded to pack her belongings quietly, eventually speaking up again.

"You don't feel safe at home either, do you?" It wasn't a question; it was a well-thought, conclusive statement she had fired straight at me. I refused to reply and shoved my math textbook into the most significant space in my bag, not for homework. Still, it was just something to decorate my desk in case my parents unexpectedly barged in at any moment of the evening.

"I'm also afraid to go home every day."

Incoming Danielle rant part two.

I had nothing against her ranting—I'm pretty relieved she feels comfortable sharing her innermost emotions with her psychotic friend—but I'm no advice provider. I hope she's okay with someone just listening to her quibbles.

"Like, the point of a home is to have a safe space to run back to, right?" She raised her head just enough to lock eyes with me. I understood every word that left her lips, but I didn't dare to communicate my feelings like she did.

I nodded to her, hoping my eyes told her I understood and could hear her clearly. She reciprocated my nod, and we both focused back on packing our bags. Actually, mine was already packed, and I was mindlessly pouring in air into my bag at that point. My ears finally picked up the sound of a closed zip, causing me to look up and watch Danielle swing her bag effortlessly over her shoulders.

"Have you ever had shoulder surgery?"

"What? No!" She blurted out, perplexed by the seemingly random question.

"Never mind." She has unbreakable bones, then.

"Anyway, it seems like the others won't return to class, as their bags aren't here." She gestured towards Chima and Olivia's seats, which looked like two abandoned pieces of land.

"I guess they took their bags to their class before lunch time."

"Seems so." Her hands dipped into her desk one last time to confirm she wasn't leaving anything behind before approaching the door.

"Anyhow sha, see you tomorrow!" I waved lightly as

she disappeared out the door, loneliness and fear stepping into my being not long after. They both gripped me tightly while I straddled my face in my palms, dreading the torment that awaited my presence at night. Just as Danielle said, my home is meant to be a place of comfort, safety, and support, yet it reflected the complete opposite of its general definition for me. I'll have to return home to endure my parents' perpetual criticism and be non-existent to my only sibling.

And that's before getting sexually abused by a paedophile. This was my life every day, once school was taken out of the equation.

"We're going home." I recognised my sister's voice from the doorway, but she disappeared as quickly as she came. Once again, I brushed off all longing feelings towards our fractured relationship and unwillingly exited the classroom.

After all, sibling rivalry wasn't the major problem in my life.

CHAPTER SIX

I Can't Have Visitors (1)

The ride home was an unsettling type of silence—as if an invisible person were holding all three of us at gunpoint and would've shot us if we uttered a word. Surprisingly, my sister's headphones weren't glued to her ears, unlike other times, signifying the gravity of the unspoken situation in the car. My mum focused solely on the road and its unskilled drivers; my sister's eyes were as empty as my mathematical set and my mind was stuck in figuring out a secret hiding spot to prevent tonight's unwanted event. For two straight months, I tried to construct a suitable hiding spot that the man could never detect, but to my dismay, he saw through it every time.

My mum increased the volume of the radio as we sped off. The voices cracked like a YouTube video with a wrong signal, and ads colonised most radio stations. They talked about the richness of Bournvita or how Milo would boost our energy by a thousand per cent. I understood that high demand equalled something (didn't pay attention during Economics class), but most brands now push their aim on 'over-exaggeration' instead of 'honesty and satisfaction'.

Although I have no right to state my opinion about any of this.

Out of desperation to enjoy a few more moments of mental sanity, I began closely observing each person's behavioural patterns. It seemed like a foolish idea, but this was my best bet compared to moping. I started by watching my mum's facial expression. Stone-hard, despairing, and possibly tired. Her shoulders seemed tense while refusing to relax, her fingers were gripping the steering tighter than usual (possibly indicating anger), her eyes remained straight for most of the ride, and her dressing style was more of a 'rushing out', rather than an 'I-took-my-time' style.

Deflecting my focus from my mother, I began observing my sister, but we unfortunately made eye contact, and her glare was enough to turn my head in the opposite direction. A forceful end to my adventurous 'observing the family' game.

"Diana." My mum's voice cut through my thoughts like a slick knife. I noticed Diana's face tense up as she replied.

"Yes, mummy?"

She resumed her silent treatment; the longer the silence, the more uncomfortable Diana felt. Her body rocked slowly on her spot, an attempt to soothe her boiling nerves as our mum continued driving in silence. I eventually sighted our house and knew the conversation would explode when we stepped through the doors.

As we drove into our gate, I noticed a human shadow lurking behind some historical trees, standing tall since the beginning of time. When the sounds from the radio no longer hit my ears, I knew we had parked, and the storm that refused to start in the car would explode in the house, shattering whatever peaceful atmosphere remained in our home. I wasted no time jumping out of the car and heading straight towards the door. My brilliant plan was to avoid the man-made disaster they were about to create starting from the entrance of our 'beloved' home.

"Good evening, daddy," I announced as I took my first stcp into the house. He waved me off, his phone capturing all the attention he could've shared with his family members.

As usual. Work.

To avoid the explosive fight that I couldn't diffuse, I quickly made my way towards my bedroom. It radiated lifeless energy from my keyless door to the barely occupied surface area, which in turn complimented the prison-like window structures with their rusting, immovable edges. I flung my bag across the room and instantly collapsed onto my newly made sheets and blanket that would be destroyed that night, allowing me to prepare new sheets and a freshly folded blanket for the next day in my spaceless closet.

"You dropped Geography?" I heard my mum shout from the ground floor. Her angry tone penetrated my walls, leaving me no choice but to listen to one of their many arguments.

"I don't want to study it."

"You've already dropped every single science-related subject! You've dropped Chemistry, Physics, and Biology, and now you go and drop Geography, too?"

"I just genuinely don't like it! Is that such a problem?"

"What exactly are you meant to become now?" I could hear her voice rising with each word she spoke.

Or rather, shouted.

"A musician? A painter? Oh! A model?!"

"I want to become an actress! I've been saying this since SS1!"

"An actress? I did not raise you for over 17 years for you to become a cartoon character!"

"That's a different type of acting!"

"And you're a different type of failure!"

The tension I felt in the car started making vivid sense to me. Academic pressure was a major element of family harmony in this part of the world, and anything lesser than doctor, lawyer, or engineer would earn you ridicule from your parents. Unless you could prove in twenty years that the passion you stubbornly pursued led to your success and not to you sleeping under the bridge, don't bother calling them "Mum" or "Dad" until you've stabilised your career and marriage life.

"An ungrateful disgrace; that is exactly what you are!" After those words, the house fell silent. I detected rushed footsteps, followed by a delicate shutting of the door to avoid further parental row. I lay flat on my bed, staring at the ceiling with nervous intensity.

"Amanda!" My mum's voice called out the same time she barged into my room, taking in the sight of her daughter lazily stretched out in bed. I instinctively flipped over as she began to fire questions at me.

"Why aren't you studying?"

"Was arranging my bed."

"What are you studying in the future?"

"Advanced Techno-Psychology." I did not know if that existed and was pretty sure it did not exist, but whatever I could make sound sweet and powerful in her ears was worth the fib.

She tilted her head in confusion, "Advanced kini?"

"Techno-Psychology. It's like physics but involves extensive studies about computer-mind stuff." She nodded to the nonsense I sprouted out to form reasonable sentences. I was grateful it wasn't my dad I was having this awkward, uneasy conversation with because he could spin you into a cycle while you're trying to fool him. He reverses what you're throwing at him before it hits him, like playing baseball and him being the batter.

"That's good. One of my daughters future is still bright." The tension in my mum's shoulders appeared to relax for the first time this afternoon. In some way, I felt for Diana: choosing a career path she loved over what our parents desired would instantly make her an outcast in the family, and that didn't sit right with me. We had never been sisterly, but that didn't make me necessarily hate her or her aspiration callously condemned.

Besides, it wasn't as if my future was very bright either way, not with my nightly terrors. "Anyway," She seemed to remember why she came up the stairs in the first place, instead of expending the remaining energy in shouting my name as usual. I had a suspicious feeling it wasn't only my academics she came to question me about, so I paid rapt attention to what she was going to say.

"We'll be having a visitor next week Wednesday."

I stayed still, awaiting further information. But that seemed to be all.

"Oh, alright then," I said after the awkward pause.

"She'll be staying with us for a few days, so I'd like her to share a room with you when she arrives."

Wait… what? What?!

Part Two

CHAPTER SEVEN

I Can't Have Visitors (2)

Wait…what?!

"I hope there's no problem, this one that you're staring at me looking like crayfish." My mum scoffed impatiently.

The insult flew over my head, my mind more focused on the problem in her announcement.

"She cannot stay here!" I blurted out, staring at her and folding my arms defiantly. It was an admittedly silly move, but the determination to avoid putting someone else's life in danger was much stronger than the unexpected sleepover my mum had previously blatantly refused to accommodate since I was ten.

Each time I raised the question of a sleepover when I was younger, she'd quote, "Sleepovers can cultivate demonic actions. "The statement never made sense to me at the time: How could a friend or two sleeping over possibly lead to any demonic activity taking place in my bedroom?

She never dove deeper into her short yet blunt disapproval, which only triggered my rebellious nature to go ahead and want to do it secretly. I never actually went through with my unrealistic plans; this is an African home where no such plans are successful. I would have gotten caught within seconds.

Anyways, that was then. Right now, I have gone past wishing I could sneak friends into my room, to ensuring no soul was found in my room past 7 p.m.

"Am I addressing someone, or am I talking to myself?" My mum's voice yanked me back to the present. I blinked hard, trying to narrow in on this sudden decision of hers. She glared at me, still expecting a plausible reason for my refusal.

"She just... can't stay in... well, my room," I stammered.

Her lips fell into a deeper frown. My answer hadn't satisfied her.

"And why not?" She countered, "Do you do witchcraft in your room at night?"

My eyes widened in shock. "Of course I don't! I'm a child of God."

"You better be." I let out an inaudible sigh. Any louder and my insolence would be met with instant punishment.

"Do you smoke in your room at night?"

"Mummy, have you ever entered my room in the

morning and perceived smoke?"

"Ehn, maybe you open the window while doing it, "she continued to probe.

Surely she cannot be serious right now. I wouldn't dare touch a cigarette, even if it were a life-or-death situation (although smoking could technically lead to my death anyway). It was a vow I had made to myself ever since I saw a newly printed flier dangling off the rusty electricity poles hammered into the ground by each side of our rowdy road. I had been leaning against the car window, eyeing the poop that a mischievous bird had left on the glass, before catching sight of the flier that boldly read.

'If You Smoke, You'll Get a Stroke.'

Ironically, three middle-aged men were smoking right under that flier, so I was pretty sure the majority of smokers did not care about having a stroke. They must all be rich and be able to afford medical bills quickly.

"Mummy, I do not smoke!" I retorted bravely.

"Ok, o, if you say so." My lips formed a thin line while I awaited her next illogical accusation.

"Ehen!" She exclaimed, her eyes lighting up as her mind settled on a false realization. "You have a secret boyfriend, abi?"

A boyfriend. Ha! I wish I were in a better mental state so I could roll my eyes at her words while laughing uncontrollably. If my mother thought I could sneak boys into my room in the middle of the night, then I needed to give her more credit for being humorous. There are three unimpeachable reasons why this assumption of hers could never happen: Number one: African home. Number two: African Home. Number three: African Home.

See? It's never happening, not in this country.

My furrowed brows told her that it was none of those things, and she tapped her feet with growing impatience, waiting for me to give her a suitable answer.

"If it's not what I listed above, why can she not stay in your bedroom?"

I bit my lips as I shot out the first sentence that popped into my brain, which I instantly regretted the moment it made it through my lips. "I pee on the bed."

I saw the shock waves run through her body, her feet unconsciously recoiling from me. "You still weewee on the bed?" she asked incredulously.

"Yes, mummy," I replied to her, lowering my gaze.

Her fingers stroked her chin lightly. "No wonder you're always changing your sheets daily. Chai, as big as you are." She rolled her eyes at my confession. I knew that the lie would embarrass me for years, and I could already envision her typing away on her Facebook page, appealing to members of her prayer group to assist her in casting out demons of bedwetting from her younger daughter.

"How about Diana's room?" I started to suggest it mainly because of the heightened level of embarrassment that engulfed me.

"My friend, will you shut up your mouth!" The anger she had barely suppressed since her blowup with Diana now threatened to erupt again. I knew that the moment she left my room, she would storm into Diana's.

I kept looking at my feet while she eyed me from head to toe. Eventually she sighed and said, "Oh well. I cannot let my guest sleep in a room when my daughter wets the bed every day. How disgraceful."

She didn't bother to conceal the disgust that took over her face as she contemplated why she bothered with me in the first place. Without so much as a dismissal, she marched out of my room and left the door wide open like a typical African mother to whom children's personal spaces were a myth. As I imagined, a thunderous pounded echoed from the hallway. If I had placed a bet on her action after leaving my room, I would have been showered in dollars right now.

"Open this door before I break it!" I heard her growl. I cautiously pushed my bedroom door shut, praying that her ears didn't translate it as a disrespectful slam. Fortunately, she seemed pretty preoccupied with ripping my sister's barricade apart.

I instantly slumped towards the unwelcoming floor, my back blocking further entrance into my room. I spiralled into an ocean of thoughts, heavily grateful that I had succeeded in preventing another human from experiencing this traumatic contamination. But then it occurred to me that maybe the presence of another individual was actually the solution to this depressing cycle.

Or perhaps the molester would have the pleasure of seizing another person's virginity, if she was still a virgin, that is.

"Just a year and some months more to go." In my absurdity, counting the days until the handcuffs were taken off me was much more convenient than simply reporting this heartbreaking occurrence. But I was not brave enough to take that step and preferred not to draw pitiful attention to myself.

Or maybe, in fact, the actual reason was because no one would take my statement seriously in the first place.

The ball of fire in the sky slowly began to fall, and the blinding orange horizon slipped through my worn window bars, settling perfectly onto my crumpled green sheets and matching blanket. I remained glued to my butt-aching position, drowning myself in the beautiful clash of rich orange rays colliding with the bright lemonade tinge of the clouds. My translucent curtains danced with the occasional breeze hitting their bodies, forming curvy waves on the patternless fabrics.

I shifted my gaze towards my closet, situated at one of

the furthest corners of my spacious bedroom. Isolated from all other furniture in the room, yet it still made such a huge impact when shielding all my private area covers from the rest of the world, including my exceptionally nosy mother. It was quite an unexciting arrangement I had created, mainly consisting of a medium-sized bed parallel to the room's entrance, boring curtains barely blocking the view of the window bars, my book dumpsite for a desk, and lastly, the closet, which had space only to keep clothes and probably only a new-born baby could fit inside its rooms.

There are no hiding spots for me though. It seemed like all corners of my room were widely visible, which didn't bother me before—the thought of hiding from someone had never really occurred to me until that particular night. I also started wishing I wasn't tidy; maybe having a dump of a room would've caused havoc for my unwanted nightly visitor.

But I have an African mother. Not just African, but a Nigerian mother. My room in an upside-down state certainly won't last long with her cleaning addiction.

'I do not raise barbarians,' she frequently remarked.

Noticing that my butt had now begun to ache unbearably, I finally lifted myself off the ground. The word soap flashed through my mind, loudly spoken by a particular teacher earlier today.

"I don't even care anymore," I mumbled, dragging my

floppy body towards the bedside.

Not even a minute had passed before a booming voice blasted through the walls. "Diana and Amanda, you better come downstairs to eat dinner o! I don't want anyone entering my kitchen past 8 p.m.!"

Shocking. She had somehow teleported from my sister's bedroom to the ground floor in a matter of, oh wow! Thirty minutes. I didn't realize I had been on the floor for that long. How time flies when you're zoned out from reality.

"These children, will you come downstairs?!" My mum called out again.

I imagined that their conversation didn't last for long because I didn't hear any slap sounds or an accompanying yell. But then, I was far removed from their altercation at the time to detect any slap sounds (maybe because I left Earth throughout their entire conversation).

Considering that only the top half of my body was lying on the comfort of my mattress, I decided there was no point in not heading downstairs for dinner. My digestive system had proven that it wouldn't accept anything I fed it.

"Ekomamwen! Igiósé!"

Clearly, my mother's impatience had spiked to record levels because she had switched to our native names, a rare   occurrence.

"Oh well, down we go," I told myself as I gathered all

my strength to get through to my feet. In five reluctant steps, I was out of my room. After about twenty more hesitant steps, I was in the dining room. Another three, and I was beside my usual seating spot.

After looking around, I noticed that our dad was no longer on his working couch. He frequently disappeared about this time and spent more time getting to work commitments in his beloved car than bonding over a family dinner. I didn't mind because it meant one less unreasonable parent to deal with.

"So I had to call your names over ten times before you people could come downstairs, abi?" What's my mother if she wasn't over-exaggerating?

My sister fixed her gaze at our family portrait hanging beside the curtains, her eyes firing off silent darts and looking as red as lava. I wondered why that particular photograph was still displayed when it was over ten years ago. Why do visitors have to see me in that young state with several of my teeth missing?

"You better go and serve yourselves. Me, I am not your maid," she hissed as she wiped off her hands on a napkin.

"Ok, ma." We chorused.

"Also, I have decided that the visitor will be staying in the guest room since the both of you are not mature enough to take care of a guest as teenagers." I remained expressionless as she shook her head at us.

Isn't that where visitors were supposed to stay in the first place?

How did she even forget we had a guest room? How did I forget that we had a guest room?

"And you." Her fingers invasively pointed at my sister, whose eyes did not blink despite the rounded fingernail a mere three inches from poking them. "Our talk isn't over. We'd continue that discussion tomorrow."

She didn't wait for Diana's response and grabbed her substantial blue flask from the centre table before climbing the stairs up to her room. As soon as she was out of eyeshot, I pushed my chair away from the table.

"And where are you going?" Diana shot at me accusingly.

"Anywhere but the kitchen," I replied dryly, inserting the chair back into the table now that I was standing up. "She called us downstairs to eat," Diana said in the same tone.

I didn't look at her as I replied, "It doesn't look like you're planning on eating either." She hissed at me but followed my lead in leaving the table. I ignorantly dismissed her apparent hypocrisy and walked towards the living room. My eyes fell on our square-shaped clock, which, instead of numbers, had long and short lines to indicate the hours and minutes.

Night was slowly approaching, and I tried to enjoy every last bit of my time before he showed up.

"I'm staying in the living room, by the way!" I heard Diana shout from behind.

I rolled my eyes and sighed sardonically. Calling dibs on the living room was such a childish thing to do.

"Really, Diana?" I said to her.

"Just go somewhere else!" She snapped as she glided past me, quickly snatching the remote control from the couch before I had a chance to reach it first. Not in the mood to extend this pointless argument, I reversed course and headed back to the dining room.

"So, you've finally decided to eat?" She called out mockingly, her animated voice letting me know it was a statement, not a question.

"I'm just going to sit down and stare until I become a psychopath." I drawled, still trying to avoid an argument but irritated by her barbs.

"Weirdo." Even she couldn't help herself.

Well, she isn't wrong. I certainly am a certified weirdo.

CHAPTER EIGHT

I Hate My Reality

"Mmm...that was fun."

He groaned while slowly buttoning up his shirt. I was frozen in my dimly lit room as I drenched my once pure sheets with my waterfall of tears. I struggled to close my legs, but the unbearable pain paralyzed my legs in their current awkward position. My heart was pumping frantically and only beat faster with each passing second.

He did it again. He took what was mine effortlessly, and it felt as though I never even attempted to put up a decent fight. But he had a height that completely dwarfed me, arms that seemed like they could easily hoist multiple bags of cement at the same time, and his gaze frightening enough to make an onion sob. A heartless human machine—that's exactly who he is.

Ripples of shivers ran down my body as I felt rough fingers graze the side of my throbbing neck.

"I can't wait for tomorrow, my beautiful toy." Those last three words stung harder than a bee could ever have.

He didn't bother to mask his impatience at the thought of violating me again the following day, yet he planted a light kiss on my neck. I shuddered when his lips touched my skin, and he chuckled lightly.

"You're so sexy," he drawled, as if that should make me feel good. I didn't dare utter a word, anxiously waiting for his breath to disappear from my side.

The hot breath finally shifted away from my neck, and a brief feeling of relief washed over me. Sadly, it couldn't wash away the sickening tattoo his actions had marked all over me—initiated through force and not fair will—staining even my unconscious state of mind. I remained still in pain, too frightened to make any move that could lure him back towards my body. His steps drew further away until I could hear the familiar squeak of the door as it pulled open.

Finally, a closing click reached my ears, and his footsteps transformed from light taps into still silence. Air rushed out of my lungs like that of a marathon runner, but my heart continued to race and refused to slow down. The sheets beneath me were covered in goo, a combination of a sticky substance that my mind refused to process and pools of tears from my eyes. My body wished for an escape, perhaps to fall into a trance, but I knew sleep wasn't an option. Scenes from this traumatic event will play over in my mind continuously until the sun comes up.

I glanced briefly at the clock before my eyes fell back down, facing my isolated wardrobe. In my mind, I saw it looking at me pitifully from its immobile position, wishing that it could have saved me from the monster if only it had a much bigger hiding spot within it. 'Not your fault', I muttered through my streaming tears. I couldn't care less if my quiet pity party was with a non-living item, as long as I had someone, or in this case, something, who bore witness to my agony.

As I resumed my attempts at closing my immobilized legs, I silently began to question my faith. It was weird being trapped under the spell of a human demon, yet no angels had flown in to beat him up for hurting his child. Realistically, I wasn't expecting angels to finish him off, but at least something—a sign, even—could've shielded me from this unwanted experience.

Maybe I wasn't as spiritually strong as my mother or father.

Maybe I didn't believe hard enough?

Maybe he's busy with other problems.

Sigh. None of my questions had answers.

None of my questions had answers!

I cried out in pain as sharp, precise pains shot through my veins once more, halting my legs' attempt to reunite. Just as my mind quickly flew into my faith questions, it similarly swiftly dashed to much darker thoughts that were perfectly in tune with the physical and mental torment.

I was just an average, ordinary, obedient (well, some-times) teenager who had avoided any source of trouble for the past fifteen years. Yet somehow, I got forcefully plugged into the one source from which I diligently and deliberately steered clear. Every day, I chanted in my brain, 'No, Until Marriage! No, Until Marriage!'

And yet, I still got my precious, unique, priceless virginity stolen from me!

Even after carefully hammering all the warnings I've received from when I could barely pronounce words till my teenage years (with the strict tones of all mothers, teachers, adults, and elders that occupy this land remind-ing me daily to never engage in an action that could lead me to multiply at such a young age), I ended up getting thrown into the pit of ferocious lions, into the world of heartless monsters that lack decency and respect, which are replaced by an overwhelming amount of cruelty towards unsuspecting victims.

For human beings that intake oxygen like the rest of the world to process and execute such physical and emotional damage to their kind, they are only coated with one layer, unlike the rest of us. They have a body but lack a wholesome spirit and a soul. Or it's possible that the demons in charge of them have now expelled both from their beings, leaving them empty vessels for their wicked purposes.

The sudden sound of a closing door snapped me out of my sorrowful daze, making me impulsively jump out of bed despite the growing ache that racked through my body.

"Who is awake?" Oh no. That voice was too loud, too familiar, and way too close to my door, which means:

"Amanda oo, have you not slept?" No.

No no no no no no! My mum cannot see me like this!

As my door handle bent slowly, I flung myself back in bed, forcing my eyes shut while the repulsive smell from my duvet rushed up my nose. It was like fighting a world war underneath my bed sheets—from guns firing around my abdomen to a row of bombs exploding down my intestines. I couldn't identify which part had an ally or was an enemy, but I certainly understood the pain the world felt when the world wars took place.

"Is she sleeping?" She questioned herself suspiciously. I could feel her eyes piercing through my duvet, scanning for even the slightest detail that could give me away.

Don't move, don't move, don't move! I kept chanting as my eyelids struggled to keep up the act. I was also silently praying that her sense of smell wasn't working correctly, and if it did, she'd probably think I'd 'let it go' on my bedsheets again while I was sleeping. That would probably make her pray harder for me to be delivered from the demons of bedwetting.

"Ok, she's asleep. I thought I heard sounds from this

room." Phew, that was a close one. She then sauntered off, her housecoat sweeping the floor softly.

The cold air that rushed in from the world outside my bedroom didn't feel as strong anymore, meaning I had missed the sound of my door closing. Still, it also told me she was finally a thousand miles away from figuring out that a sexually-driven man had dominated whatever peaceful energy was previously present in this room.

I wanted to know what time it was, so I made plans to gather myself. I groaned as I turned and dangled just off the side of the bed. The pain had resurfaced, and so had the upcoming vomit, which I desperately tried to hold in. I balanced my body gingerly, willing the impulse away until I was able to calm the storm in my belly. My strained backbone paid the price for holding still in that position.

I sighted my phone at the edge of my study desk, but my body let me know instantly that there was no miraculous way to walk or crawl such a distance with the horror my body was experiencing. As I retreated to my flat position, my head landed on a cold, miniature device. I mustered up the strength in my arms to reach the back of my head, whipping out my analogue watch that I could thankfully read. A dim ray of light shone perfectly on its face and I tried to make out the two ticking hands in an attempt to know the time.

"12:30; just four hours and 30 more minutes until the

night is over," I uttered breathlessly. Then I began to weep quietly, shedding tears that no one could, would, and must never see.

CHAPTER NINE

A Typical Morning (1)

4:57.

4:58.

4:59.

5:00.

"Oya, it's time for school; wake up!" As always, right on time. I slowly turned my neck away from the wall, willing myself towards my energetic mother. She entered noiselessly and immediately began to bang on my table in rhythmic beats, like a professional traditional drummer who needed to show off her skills so that everyone could witness her talent.

Well, I am not everyone; I am not a crowd, and my bedroom is certainly not a village square. Right now, all she's doing is magnifying my headache.

Her voice called out impatiently, "My friend, will you get up and get ready for school?" Thankfully, she stopped banging on my desk.

I remained motionless while I fixed my eyes on her, eyeing her zebra-patterned hair bonnet and plain orange nightdress down to the slippers, one of the pairs she haggled over at the market before buying. She looked like a regular housewife, but nothing about her was regular.

"Can you not hear me?" Her tone increased, signalling to me that she was becoming irritated with my laziness. "I'm getting up now!" I replied quickly before her irritation turned into full-blown anger. I let out a fake yawn while she added one of her "back in the day" stories to illustrate why we kids nowadays supposedly 'have it easy'.

"I always trekked to school. And before I went to school, I would sweep my entire house, wash plates, and then sweep the neighbour's front yard. But I have to wake up before you and still have to wake you two."

She must have told this story a thousand times already, and it never made sense to me. Firstly, what strength would I have to start sweeping at five o'clock in the morning? Secondly, why would I be sweeping the neighbour's compound, where I don't live? Even if I were such a pleasant child, why would it be my duty to do that kind of unpaid janitorial work for another family?

I sank my head back into my pillow as she continued grumbling.

"Unlike me, you children are still asleep at this time. If I did not come and call you now, you'll sleep until nine."

I chuckled internally. Sleep? No. Thinking about my life and its downturn? Absolutely.

After a few more seconds, it seemed like she ran out of reflective comments this morning, and she gestured again at me to leave the bed before finally leaving my room, pulling the door close behind her.

"At least she shut the door this time," I muttered, gathering up the ability to lift myself from the damp bed. It felt like there were hundreds of pins and needles piercing through my skin and body, and attempting to stand aggravated the pain I'd been feeling but concealed throughout my mum's combative pep talk.

In fairness, her speech wasn't necessarily a bad thing, but she typically didn't notice anything around her when she started to sermonize in the morning, which is why she must not have been hit by the musky smell emanating from my sheets. On the other hand, it was surprising that she didn't add a bible verse to drive home her point about our purported lack of responsibility. One time, she quoted John 3:16 while playing a worship soundtrack in the background. As she refused to download a bible app because she thought smartphones didn't carry the same spiritual power as an actual bible, she read from a miniature version she carried in the pocket of her housecoat all the time. I remember wondering what the point of God telling us He gave His only son to us was. What did that have to do with sweeping and doing house chores?

"Are you still on that bed? I hope you're not still on that bed!" Her voice floated through the concrete walls, forcing my thoughts aside so I could reply in a coherent tone.

"No, ma, I'm about to have my bath!"

"Better remove that bedsheet as well, o!"

Oh God. So, she did perceive a smell! Although she obviously interpreted it as the embarrassing lie I had told her yesterday. Regardless, she smelled something!

"Did you hear me?!"

"Yes, ma!" I managed to reply audibly before she launched into another tirade about bedwetting at my age. With her ringing voice, it was sure that my dad and sister could hear her as well. That was an extra layer of trouble I wasn't ready to deal with this early.

I took a look at the lower part of my body, scanning my trembling legs and my arms wrapped around my unsettled stomach. A salty droplet slid down my cheek, and that's when I realized I had already taken a bath.

In my sweat.

I took a few moments to gather some composure and keep my throat from impulsively giving way to the bile gathering in my stomach, then I managed to stand straight without collapsing. My braided hair felt like torture as it rubbed against the back of my neck, and the early morning cold swept around my feet, so I slipped them into my worn-out crocs. They were a trusty pair, but

I refused to change them for new ones, even after having multiple chances to do so. They might have been old, but they were more comfortable than anything else I owned.

I flicked on the light switch, and the room was bathed in bright, fluorescent light. It provided a much-needed expulsion from the gloomy darkness, yet it was lifeless and uncomforting. The atmosphere was stifling, and in the quiet of the morning, the miser hung low like a soggy carpet. I stood in the same spot, wondering if moving a little bit would make me splat all over the ground like a cartoon character. Will I instantly turn into a liquid that no scientist could ever identify? Will I ultimately acquire the forbidden power of shape-shifting? If so, I'd love to shape-shift into a pair of scissors and mercilessly cut off that man's-

"It's almost 5:30 o!" came from downstairs. Right. I forgot I was supposed to be preparing for school.

My eyes bounced around the room, searching for the toilet door that seemed elusive, making me move my head left and right repeatedly, as if I were about to cross the road. The urge to barf began to reassemble towards my oesophagus, and I was almost in the bathroom when a soft ping went off on my phone.

"Who could that be?" I wondered wordlessly while picking the phone off my desk. The glaring light made me flinch, and I squinted to be able to make out the text on the phone. I saw the name 'Olive' at the top of the

WhatsApp message list.

DIRECT MESSAGE WITH OLIVE.

Amandaaaaa! (5:32 a.m.) [Olive]

What? (5:32 a.m.) [Me]

This is important! (5:32 a.m.) [Olive]

We can chat in school. (5:32 a.m.) [Me]

I can't find my tieee!! (5:32 a.m.) [Olive]

How did you lose your tie in your house? (5:32 a.m.) [Me]

That's the thing! I didn't! [Olive]

I remember wearing it at home, but I don't remember having it on when I changed yesterday! (5:32 a.m.) [Olive]

Just check your house well (5:32 a.m.) [Me]

I literally checked everywhere! (5:32 a.m.) [Olive]

Then check harder (5:33 a.m.) [Me]

I did!! (5:33 a.m.) [Olive]

Then check again. [Me]

I'm going to go now; see you at school. (5:33 a.m.) [Me]

Urgh! You're not helping at all!! (5:33 a.m.) [Olive]

Typical Olivia. She actually texted me because she couldn't find her tie. I shook my head at the banality of the exchange and placed the phone back on the desk. "Some people don't have problems," I said to myself, shuffling into the bathroom. Taking a shower is such a mundane routine, but it's necessary to do it so that people don't turn their heads at you for all the wrong reasons. At least I managed to brush my teeth and shower once a day.

Until last week, I could only see the sink and the toilet bowl in this small space. Since then, they have become the place of respite after each night. I couldn't wait to scrape the repulsion away from my tongue with the stinging taste of toothpaste.

But then, why does Close-up always taste like medicine mixed with pepper?

"6 a.m.! Everyone downstairs!" My mum commanded from the dining room.

Does time really fly this fast?

Has time ever flown this fast?

With little time left to think, I carried out my only sanitary routine as quickly as my body allowed me to. In no time, I was buttoning up my barely white shirt, eyeing the skirt that I desperately wished could turn into trousers.

Maybe then he wouldn't have noticed my body.

Sigh. I couldn't prevent my thoughts from drifting there.

"Diana, are you still sleeping?! It's 6am!" My mum was a stickler for time and yelled at Diana. I didn't realize she was still in bed.

"Thank God there's another sibling in the house she can shout at," I thought to myself. If I was the only child, my parents won't have their mental sanity anymore. I would've either been locked up in a mental institution or probably sacrificed back to God in exchange for a new child.

Like my Crocs, my school shoes were well-worn, and I slipped my feet in, still holding myself back from retching. Then I absently snatched my bag from beside my reading chair. I shook it for a while before stuffing two outdated textbooks into the largest zip compartment. My father had begun to question what my school bag was for since it was mostly empty except for a couple of books and biscuit crumbs. Textbooks were hand-me-downs from Diana, but it didn't bother me if they were stained, damaged, or had lost a couple of pages. It was a textbook, as long as it still had at least one page filled with boring nonsense.

"You're finally out of your room." Those words were fired at me the moment I stepped out the door.

"I was dressing up," I replied dryly.

"I hope you removed your bedsheet," she continued.

Aha! That. I knew I was forgetting something.

My mother gave me a final look before returning her attention to Diana's room door. She continuously banged—more like punched—on it, demanding to know what was keeping her in there.

"Probably doing a pointless skin-care routine," I muttered, dashing into my room to rip out the soiled sheets. When I got downstairs, my father was in his usual position. This morning, he had a new pair of glasses on his face, peering at the equally newly purchased laptop computer.

"So, you cannot greet," he grumbled.

"Good morning, Sir." No reply.

It had become our daily ritual: him not waiting for me to greet him before accusing me of not greeting, me offering the greeting, and him ignoring it. His coldness did nothing to me anymore, and his standoffishness breezed by me harmlessly. I was used to it. I headed towards the laundry, skipping over a scampering wall gecko in the damp room, and threw my sheets beside the washing machine. It seemed to have more of a purpose than I did at that moment; at least it was desired for its usefulness in washing our clothes and always having a fresh, newly-washed scent while I felt anything but clean.

I wish we could switch places right now.

After mockingly laughing at myself for starting to become jealous of an inanimate item, I returned to the dining area. I sat parallel to my father, wringing my bag onto the ground. He didn't flinch, and he kept his attention on whatever business deal he was conducting virtually. The HP logo on the back of his laptop caught my eye, and I mindlessly watched the colour switch from neon blue to bleak grey. It was a nice distraction: the flashing lights, his mountain of leadership books, the fact that he was already wearing a suit at 6:40 a.m., his bruised knuckles, his—

Wait.

I did a double-take and looked again at his knuckles.

'Dried blood, peeled skin, reddish, stiff finger joints, as if he punched someone.'

Or something…

What exactly happened when he left the house yesterday? Did he get into fisticuffs with a colleague? Or maybe his boss?

But why would he punch his boss?

Did he even punch his boss?

Why do I think he punched his boss? It could've been a wall.

But he's not generally a violent person, that is, if we exclude all the 'holy deliverance' he did for us with the anointing power of his belt from ages two to ten.

"Mummy, I was already ready! I just fell back asleep. "The clashing sounds of my mother and sister arguing back-to-back interrupted my questioning thoughts. My father's head remained down, focused on his devices only.

"So, all the time I was banging on your door, you didn't hear me, abi?"

"I didn't hear you!" Diana could match my mother's vocal pitch, and she didn't back down easily.

"That's a lie! You were pretending not to hear me." My mum continued, determined to have the last word.

Diana groaned in annoyance, aggressively popping her bottle open and smashing it into the water dispenser. But my mum wasn't done and pushed even more. "Do you know what time it is? Your dad could have been taking you to school by now."

Diana didn't give in either. She cocked her neck to glare at my mum, "It's just 6:42 a.m.!"

"JUST 6:42? You are late!" This was the opening mum was looking for, and she lashed out fiercely. "It is this delaying spirit of yours that's delaying your brain. That's why you chose a stupid career."

Oh look, my dad's head finally rose to take in the scene happening in front of him. What a miracle.

The tension that engulfed our house was palpable. It could be felt, smelled, touched, or even strangled. Diana had only filled half of her bottle, yet she froze and tightly clenched it. My dad was carefully assessing the situation, his eyes darting from my mum to my sister and to his computer screen. A rueful look briefly flashed across my mum's face but it was quickly replaced by anger and stubbornness.

While my mum's relationship with me was one of indiscipline, my sister and mother always had an on-and-off relationship. Mainly off, as their quarrels had outweighed all the sweet moments and their disagreements grew more frequent these days. They were shouting over Diana's preferred school activities, her reluctance to do house chores, her prospective life choices—basically anything she was involved with—or they were exchanging gist and chatting away by themselves.

But that didn't stop my mother's apparent lack of censorship. She said whatever was on her mind with no filter and was never apologetic for it. So at times, when Diana wasn't being recalcitrant, our mother would still find something to criticize her about.

Finally, my dad had enough. "Everyone just get inside the car," he demanded firmly, breaking off my mum and my sister's unyielding eye contact.

Eventually, my mum noticed me looking on. "Amanda, have you eaten? She asked, waving my sister off like a pesky fly.

"Yes, I have." Better than telling her the truth. This wasn't the time to go through the seven stages of vomiting. Six of them were built-up nausea, and the last one was indigestion.

"OK then," she said. "Diana, get something to eat." And with that, she turned on her heel and headed towards the laundry room, leaving my sister seething next to the water dispenser. I avoided her gaze while grabbing my bag and following my dad towards his car.

"Heartless woman." I heard her murmur under her breath before shutting the front door. I understood how she felt, but our relationship was too strained for me to go over and offer her any unsolicited support.

As my dad opened the driver's car door, I glanced at his bruised knuckles again before entering the car. My sister was taking her time, so I observed them silently while he scrolled through his WhatsApp messages. I continued pondering what the story behind his knuckles was, but I didn't dare ask. "He probably already informed his wife about it, so it's none of my business," I concluded, attempting to convince myself of my mature and put-together mindset.

I relaxed into my seat, feeling my dark thoughts emerge around my brain to jolt the sadness in my soul. I looked down with a deep breath and spotted a long, strange object by the side of my seat. In the half-light of the dawn, I couldn't make out what exactly it was. I felt spooked, but my curiosity took over, and I reached for it. Before I could touch it or get a good look at it, my sister came running out of the house with my mum on her heels. "Will you get inside that car now!?"

"Ugh!" Diana groaned loudly as she settled into her seat and glared out the window. My unbothered dad continued to reverse. I started to float towards my daily nightmares and soon forgot the strange object.

CHAPTER TEN

A Typical Morning (2)

"Why would she give us six questions to do?! And great! They have babies and grandchildren each!" Math class had commenced, and my friend Olivia had a complaint.

"Like... a, b, c?" I asked monotonously.

"Yes, a, b, c, all the way to z."

"Now you're exaggerating, Olivia." Danielle pitched in.

"But didn't she give us homework just yesterday?" Olivia whined while anxiously flipping through her textbook.

Danielle sighed, her hand rummaging through her bag for her government notepad, "What are you going to do? Start a no-more-homework protest?"

"Wait, can we actually do that?"

"No, you idiot!"

A baby growl escaped Olivia's lips as she flung her textbook aside and collapsed onto the floorboards. Her head lazily leaned against my desk as she began to pout and grumble, imitating a child deprived of candy. Arms firmly folded, cheeks puffing out, and the classic puppy dog eyes that no one falls for. Although the sight and smell of her luscious box, and bra-length braids somehow enhanced her entire cutesy act.

My cheeks remained flat on my desk; their surface had been hardened by harmattan. My sight danced between Danielle and Olivia, as they were the only two people my position allowed me to see clearly. Danielle was still tirelessly searching for her government note while Olivia continued her pointless pouting at the side of my table. I glanced down at her, eyeing the prohibited yellow scrunchy, fancy school boots, and her skirt, which she had forced a slit into. Her fashion sense was spectacular, but she was implementing it in the riskiest outfit.

Her uniform.

She was the definition of an innocent rebel. The girl who glided down the hallways, beaming and sending sweet greetings towards her classmates and teachers, was the same girl whose entire outfit and attitude were at odds with school rules. It was an exciting part of being her friend. Watching adults get smitten and pissed at her was one of the few entertaining parts of being at school. Her cute yet sassy attitude must be another reason she hasn't unfriended me yet, and I couldn't just fling her out of my life for some reason. She was basically glitter, never completely leaving your life, regardless of how often you wash it off.

"I'm shocked our teacher isn't here yet, Danielle." Olivia finally spoke, breaking the silence that swarmed only us.

"Same here. Obviously, Amanda isn't going to class like Chima, but our teacher should've been here by now."

"Glad you know me so well." Danielle snickered before violently ripping open my bag and digging through my only two textbooks. Olivia stared at her, her eyes filled with confusion.

"I'm also shocked you lost your note. Aren't you the most responsible student in the class?" Danielle shifted her attention from my near-empty bag and began eyeing Olivia in the calmest way possible.

She wasn't wrong, though. Danielle was the class' free back-to-school store. She always had extra pens, erasers, rulers, and even extra math sets. Her notes and textbooks were always arranged alphabetically, wrapped in glistening wrapping paper with her name and assigned subject on top of each book. It was practically impossible for her to misplace something; her things stood out conspicuously.

"Well, at least someone would easily spot it out for me. Can't say the same about your 'tieless' neck."

"It went missing! Like someone magically stole it from me!" Danielle and I both rolled our eyes as Olivia resumed her pouting.

"How could your tie just vanish?" Danielle asked before Grace suddenly appeared beside Danielle. Her eyes judged my appearance, turning up her nose and fanning herself to clear all the pungent around me.

She mumbled something I heard clearly but wasn't sure the others heard: "Can't believe you hang out with someone who reeks of sadness and fish." Her ventriloquism needed more work if she thought I couldn't hear her. Plus, that was the lamest insult I've ever received.

She waved happily at Olivia, who rebuffed her in response to her dig at me. I was silently grateful that I had someone who looked out for me because she was now cursing Grace under her breath as she repositioned herself near my desk.

It's funny how her name certainly did not complement her obnoxious character. Her name sounds poetic and calming—a name that could soothe your tears and heal all wounds—yet the bearer was the exact embodiment of a pretentious snake that stood before us in her sad attempt at intimidating me.

Danielle was now focused on the notebook Grace had in her hands. Her lips curled into a victorious smile while Grace still tried to gain Olivia's attention like a desperate dog.

"Um, I'm guessing that's my book?" Danielle asked rhetorically, smoothly slipping the notebook out of Grace's grip.

"Ah, yes! I saw it under Michelle's desk and knew instantly it was yours." Of course, you did.

"Sorry, Danielle!" A loud alto voice conquered Grace's sheepish squeaks.

"I was using it to copy the note Mr. Akpan gave us last week! I forgot to return it to you."

Danielle just shrugged and waved off her apology. She was content that her notebook returned to her in one piece and that Olivia had no more arsenal against her.

"At least I found my note; someone is still missing her tie." Light hisses escaped Olivia's teeth, causing Danielle to laugh out of her lungs.

"Oh, Olivia! I can help you find your tie."

"My friend, will you disappear from this place? I don't need your help out of all people."

Grace's eyes thinned and became clouded with anger and jealousy. She wasn't the type to have her pride cruelly trampled on, and she did maintain a friendly disposition towards most people in school, but having Olivia, her first role model, ridicule her like that dissolved all the respect she previously had for her.

It was fascinating to see her emotions flip from polite to combative in a matter of seconds. It reminded me of how quickly my feelings could switch. The difference was that hers changed from fake to true colours, while mine switched from fake to help me!

"It's my fault for talking to you people. Rubbish." My

friends laughed loudly as Grace hissed and walked off. I was not that entertained; I just found her entire performance needlessly petty.

"Ignoring the pitiful yet oddly beneficial distraction," the words slipped through my lips in a whisper, but thankfully, they both had razor-sharp hearing. "Don't you have a spare tie, though?"

Olivia's shoulders slumped down in defeat, and her fingers messed around with what used to be white socks. "I never had a spare," she began, her hands moving from her socks towards her empty neck. "My mum just purchased one and told me to be extra careful with it."

"Well, you'll now be a tieless senior for the rest of your years at this school. Luckily, it's not that long until we're out of here. You'd survive!"

And that was enough for Olivia to snap. She reeled off an impromptu speech from her reclined position, outlining all her fantasy statistics and percentages, pointing to the favourable odds of retrieving her tie from the mysterious thief who pilfered it.

Her determination was countered by Danielle's neutral attitude, who kept re-scanning Olivia with her eyes as if she were searching for something hidden between her clothes—like those airport authorities ensuring you weren't smuggling drugs with your trousers or an over-stuffed bra.

"And lastly, it is my tie! It'll surely find its way to its

owner." The yawn that tumbled out of Danielle's mouth gave the much-needed full stop to the entire speech, and thankfully, Mr. Akpan's iconic whistling sealed the resolution.

"Sorry for being late!" He announced as he strutted across the classroom; his smart suit, consisting of the slick black blazer complementing the white inner vest paired with a crimson-coloured tie, lifted heads and turned necks. He only wore suits every week from Monday to Friday, yet he still caught his students and his colleagues' attention whenever he walked by. He was one of those people with charismatic and attractive auras.

Now, that aura was competition for attention with Danielle's flashy notebook.

"What exactly happened, sir?" She questioned as she unconsciously started heading towards her desk like the dedicated student that she was.

"I had an urgent meeting with the headmaster. He needed me to print some files for him." He calmly stationed his laptop on the teacher's desk, eye contact still firm on Danielle's.

"Sir, what were the documents for?"

"Aproko! Must you know?" The entire class burst out laughing, including Mr. Akpan himself. Danielle rolled her eyes, hissed, and settled into her seat with a strict posture. Olivia finally used her legs and lifted herself from slouching. She wiggled her body to shift her bones back into their proper places, as if there were an invisible chiropractor behind her.

"Bola, what is your problem?" She snapped at him as she rubbed Danielle's back. The gesture might have been unnecessary because Danielle's stern expression didn't relax. "It's alright, class. Bola, behave yourself!" Mr. Akpan croaked while struggling to hold back further laughter. His eyes began to leak as he stumbled towards the board. The class resumed their laughter as they watched him struggle even to touch the top of the whiteboard.

"Sir! I can help you!"

"Thank you, Gloria. All of you, you're not serious." Once again, unanimous laughter.

After a smooth exchange of his marker into the palm of Gloria, the only girl who can boast of being taller than every male who attended our school, he began gracefully gliding around the giggling classroom with an inviting smile. My eyes were continuously diverted from his slides and glides to Danielle's groans at Olivia's stubborn nature. She hadn't stopped massaging her back even after the class topic had drifted from her into our teacher's inability to become a tree.

"Amanda!"

And Mr. Akpan was now towering over me.

Well, not exactly towering because he was quite diminutive, but what he lacked in height, he made up for by trying his best to look intimidating. Right now, it was not working.

"Yes, sir?" I replied calmly.

"This is not your class; you know that, right?"

Technically, it is still SS2 A&C (Arts and Commercial) proudly nailed beside the class door.

"I know, sir."

"Then why aren't you in your class again?"

Because I'd be too busy thinking about him to learn something.

"Because I forgot where my class is." Even though I knew that was the lamest excuse my mind could have thrown up, it was all my fevered brain could manage.

His eyebrows furrowed in confusion as the background noises turned into a cacophony of snorts and murmurs.

"Because you forgo— are you a new student?"

"Yes, sir."

"Funny. You've been doing this for over a month now." He awaited a counter-response, but I had none.

"Alright, off you go! Again!"

I sighed in defeat while grudgingly rummaging through my bag for something tangible I could use as a note or textbook. Eventually, I yanked out a surviving booklet; the words 'Biology' remained the last piece of the book cover.

"So, I do have it," I mumbled before reluctantly distancing myself from my seat. I quickly dusted off the invisible particles from my unironed skirt and stared at the girl who had requested my textbook the previous day. If this were to have happened over two months ago, I'd have been at her desk squeezing my textbook into her round face while chanting, 'At least I have it now' until my voice gave up on me.

Now, I envision smashing whatever pages are left in this textbook on her head.

Okay, maybe I'm becoming a violent person. But at least I know who is to blame for it.

"Amanda! I said, please leave my classroom!" Mr. Akpan pleaded as his arms continued gesturing towards the exit. I was somewhat curious about how long he could keep his arm in that impressively still position, but it was only a matter of time before he flung me out the door himself.

As I slowly approached the exit, I felt a strong tug at the edge of my skirt. With the motive of shooting a tired side-eye, my head turned 90 degrees, only to see Olivia trying to communicate indirectly with me.

I pretended to halt in my steps to pick up a random abandoned pencil perfectly positioned by Olivia's desk, giving her enough time to whisper the words in my ear. "Please help me find my tie!"

"Really? Bruh." My eyeballs rolled so hard that I

managed to incur an instant pounding headache from it.

"Hurry it up, Amanda! In the meantime, good morning, class!"

While the class chorused their jolly greetings, I loitered about the hall.

"Madam, you've lost your tie again." I heard Mr. Akpan point out the obvious.

"Siiiirrr!" The door clicked in place after Olivia's whine. Thankfully, I didn't have to witness another barrage of defence from her.

The temperature difference was noticeable, as the hallway was a humid tunnel that was stifling.

But apart from the heat, the silence was much more torturous. Classroom noises became quieter with each passing second; even the entrance I stood beside had transformed into a soundproof structure, restricting sound waves from reaching my ears. This left me with inner voices that could encourage or destroy a human's soul. They were frequent visitors, if not illegal housemates already, but simply being in this isolated area meant specific thoughts were about to begin their slideshow.

Fortunately, the ladies' washroom wasn't so far from here.

CHAPTER ELEVEN

Something's Not Right

Broken. All that my reflection constantly revealed to me was a broken and polluted girl. A girl with permanent stains plastered all over her impure skin. A girl who had lost sight of her life, purpose, and identity after a single unexpected disaster. A girl who wished that she had been murdered in her sleep that same night instead of enduring this agonizing cycle of a man continuing to devalue whatever worth her body had left.

The tears couldn't stop flowing. They mixed with the droplets of water splattered around my ashy face, causing a steady stream to spring from my eyes and make its way through my hollowed cheeks and finally onto the sink. The heaviness in my heart pushed out more and more tears, but the weight only got heavier as I continued to sob my heart out. If a person had an allocated number of tears per day, all of mine would have been exhausted in a single minute.

I couldn't tell if the lights were still on or if they had

been switched off; I couldn't even remember if the stalls were behind me or beside me. All I could see, feel, and project was pitch-black darkness wrapped in a whirlwind of anguish. The traumatic images replayed vividly in my mind, and my body relived each second of the tortuous violation. I was trapped in a mental vortex that had no estimated ending.

Flashback

"W-why me…?" I choked through the tears streaming down my cheeks. I pulled at my sheets with a titanium grip, yet my arms continued to tremble violently.

"Because you're gorgeous," he breathed lustfully. A sharp pain of terror shot through my insides, inducing a whimper in my lips. There was a suffocating stillness in the air, wrapping around my neck like a noose. "Shh darling. I won't want to wake your parents now." Each word he said shot a dart into my heart and sucked the life out of me some more.

I heard the clasp of his belt before his raspy voice rumbled, "You're just too sexy." He grinned, eyeing my wrecked body as it tried to make its way up to my bedside. I knew he was enjoying watching the effects of what he had done to me.

He's the literal embodiment of a monster. He's not even a monster; he's a demon inhabiting the body of a human.

"I know you won't report me. And even if you did, it won't stop me from seeing you." I felt his presence inch closer to me with each passing word. I feared that the rampage would start again, and I instinctively swung myself into bed, biting my lip hard as the pain permeated my system.

I felt the blood seeping through my lips, but the heat of his acrid breath in my ear was infinitely worse than that little cut.

"I always get what I want," he whispered with a soft yet authoritative tone. "And what I want is you."

Present Day

"Cry-cry baby!" Muffled laughter cut through my breakdown, forcing me to notice the two girls snickering at me. I furiously wiped away all evidence of tears on my face. I knew it was a pointless attempt, though; how does one erase the streaks of heavy weeping in under three seconds?

The girls carried on with their taunting: "Chai, as big as you are!"

"I'm guessing a boy broke her heart." The other girl snorted as she casually approached the neighbouring sink.

Despite myself in that moment, I thought about the foolishness of presuming that a boy was the cause of my tears, or that of any girl, for that matter. If a guy even managed to touch my heart, not to mention break it, they would face serious consequences. All I had to say was, 'Hey, I've been raped,' and they're in trouble. But that's not news I'm willing to share.

"Anyway, sha, are you done crying? I want to use the sink for its actual purpose." The irritation in her voice made me want to scream and strangle her. I took a few moments to compose myself, and after a short, impatient silence, I finally stopped hovering over the sink. My textbook was practically soaked when I grabbed it and gave enough space for the mean girl to use it for its so-called actual purpose. She must have thought I didn't see a lip liner in her palm, the use of which was prohibited in school.

"Are you just going to watch us or..."

"I'm leaving," I hissed before nonchalantly swinging the toilet door open, once again entering the hallway of fire.

As their giggles dissolved into another isolating spell of stillness, I decided on the spot to aimlessly wander along the corridor and restrict myself from thinking. If I could focus all my attention on the noisy, occupied classrooms and not my consistent visitor, maybe the last ten minutes of class before everyone burst out of their classrooms would be bearable.

Although it should've occurred to me that silence and a distressed mind such as mine were not a safe combination.

I stealthily peeped into the SS2 S (Science) class. Their door reeked of paint chemicals and wood shavings, which could probably be used to create a new type of scientific formula. Their class was the only quiet class on this floor. It didn't take a genius to realize that their teacher, Mr. Okoye, was the reason for the deathly silence they studied in. He was known for having an eye for each student when he was settled in a classroom. The students dubbed him "CCTV" because he was so eerie and nothing escaped him.

"You!" his voice boomed at me. Oh well. I've been caught. Again.

The last time I was caught prowling down the hallway, it was by Mrs. Ayodele, who taught literature in English. But she calmed down pretty quickly after I explained that I was heading back from the nurses' office. Hopefully, I would never encounter a nurse and a teacher together this far away from both the bathroom and my classroom. That's the worst pairing for any student.

I was thinking up defensive statements that seemed

plausible when I realized that the voice wasn't directed at me. Perhaps someone else was skipping class? Maybe. Probably.

Or, in fact, definitely.

Given the natural human tendency to be curious, I gravitated towards the edge of the wall that led to the hallway consisting of advanced laboratories and staff offices. Barely inches away from my usual hiding spot was a protruding female backside, and…

Mr Godwin?

"I told you to get him to stop his stupid antics! I told you o, I told you!" She yelled at him, her arms grabbing his navy blue T-shirt before yanking his body closer to hers. She must be a bodybuilder if she could easily drag a muscular man near her with her petite stature.

Small but mighty, as they say.

"I tried," he snapped back as he irritably unhooked himself from her firm grasp. "But did you think he would stop what he's doing all because I told him not to?"

"Well, you're his brother!" she snarled.

"That doesn't matter!" He retorted, and she hushed him quiet, a surprising about-face because she was the one screaming at him seconds ago. He paused briefly before resuming in a low tone.

"Being related to him doesn't mean he will listen to my advice. You of all people know that well enough, given your history."

"Abeg, don't bring that one up. All I know is that he must stop what he's doing before it's too late," she said as she let go of his shirt.

He still wasn't having it and grunted, "Well, then confront him about it yourself instead of making his useless problems my own."

After minutes of wordlessly glaring at each other with their respective eyes, spent from lashing out at each other, she let out a defeated breath timed perfectly with the school bell. At the sound of the majestic ringing, they departed in opposite directions, acting like busy, preoccupied colleagues who weren't just minutes ago screaming and tangling. I still couldn't identify who the woman was, which was shocking to me given my many years of studying all angles of each staff member and knowing who was who, but I could certainly tell that she wasn't a teacher.

No particular evidence, just a hunch.

"Amanda, what are you doing there?" I didn't notice Mr. Godwin had swooped in on me and was now hovering over—actually hovering, unlike you know who.

"Just got back from the toilet, sir." I replied stiffly.

"And what happened to your textbook?"

I sighed wearily, "Accidentally fell inside the toilet."

It occurred to me that I could say it fell inside the sink and it would have been fine, but it seemed like my mind preferred embarrassing scenarios to ordinarily rational ones.

"Hmm alright." I could hear the suspicion and caution through those words and knew he was trying to confirm if I hadn't just witnessed the shady conversation he and the unidentified woman were engaged in. He continued to stare at me for a few more seconds before his attention was needed elsewhere.

"You!"

Okay, now that is referring to me.

A snort followed by a light tap on my shoulder. It was Chima disrupting the bubble I lived in, and I wish he hadn't.

"You didn't come for cla— ew what happened to your textbook?"

"Toilet. Fell. Splash." The words jumped out after one another with unexpected ease, and I decided to simply go on with that mortifying lie.

"I see," he mumbled as he took a step back.

Nice one, Chima. Nice one.

"Anyways, sha, Miss Ogunnubi said she's reporting you to Mr. Okoko again."

"Ugh, tell me something that's new," I muttered. I wasn't particularly in the mood for her overbearing inquisition this afternoon. If she wanted me to become a good student again, she should solve my nighttime situation first.

But then again, I wasn't planning on telling anyone,

especially her talkative self.

"Me, I'm just worried for you, sha." Chima continued as we made our way towards our classroom, which happened to be the loudest on the floor.

"You've been acting like this since. If I had not known you since, like, JS1 now, I'd have thought you had become a snob."

"Well, I'm not forcing you to stay, "I replied tiredly.

"Oh! So, you want me to leave, abi?"

I raised my arms defensively, saying, "No o. But you can choose not to be my friend anymore."

"Please, abeg I am still your friend. I'm just worried about you." The door swung open, almost smashing into me and leaving a dent in my forehead. Grace sauntered out, glared at me with unbridled disgust, and pushed right past me while Chima got the same treatment. We both scoffed and slid into our classroom, and we were accosted by the sound of Olivia excitedly squealing the moment she saw us.

"Finally!" She sprinted from her vantage position, from which it was easy to perpetually annoy Danielle, and practically squeezed me till I felt flattened like a piece of paper.

"Let's go for a short brea- Girl, what's with your textbook!?" I groaned loudly at the embarrassment of having to answer this awkward question for the umpteenth time this afternoon.

"It fell inside the toilet," I managed to reply, and as expected, she burst out laughing.

"Chai, that's just too funny."

As Mr. Akpan exited the classroom, preceded again by Bola, who was carrying the class's notebooks to the staff room, he turned his neck to ask, "Amanda, I hope you went for your class." I shrugged off his concern without necessarily replying to him, but I knew that Miss Ogunnubi would fill him in once they all got back to the staff room, along with the rest of the teacher gossip. Quite frankly, I couldn't be bothered.

He attempted to leave a stinging parting shot, but the words didn't form fully, and he couldn't string the words together. "This your behaviour... this your behaviour is... your behaviour is just..." Brain freeze. Glitch. Memory Loss. three-in-one combo. That's what happens when you don't mind your business.

"Sir, you sound like a robot.," Bola said cheekily, almost in a faux-innocent way that cracked the rest of the class up. Bola couldn't help himself, and in those six short words, he turned the class into a comedy club where people laughed uncontrollably.

"Bola, mind yourself o!" Mr Akpan marched off furiously, with Bola trying to keep up the pace. It was one of those moments where everyone else found it funny, but I didn't. I was more irritated by the noise than the lively din. Thankfully, Olivia and Chima were too busy bickering as usual to add to this background noise, and Danielle was just shaking her head in second-hand embarrassment.

Mr. Akpan finally had his last word and directed it at Olivia. "Olivia, you better find your tie!"

"Sir, I will! It just vanished!"

"Yeah, sure, it vanished," he snorted as they turned around the corner.

"This Bola boy is not serious." Danielle yawned tiredly and cocked her head to the side as her mouth opened wide. I waited for her to get the air out of her mouth so that she could speak to me.

"Sorry." Her neck cracked back in place as she adjusted herself into a more comfortable position.

I simply waved it off and sighed, "Eh, it's cool. There is no need for an apology."

"Alright. By the way, I needed to tell you something." She paused and looked around for Chima and Olivia, but they had both headed towards the science class. She looked around some more, noticing our very occupied classmates—some trying out new dances on TikTok, others engaging in juvenile gossip, while others discussed the never-ending boy vs girl drama.

"As I was saying,"

"Who is going for short break?!" Folakemi interjected proudly while gesturing towards our door, which was gaping open.

"I don't have money o! Who will sponsor me?"

"I think I'm going!"

"Ore are you coming with me?"

"David and Justin, let's go jor!"

One after the other, students flew through the door like birds that had just been set free from captivity. I looked back at Danielle, who seemed to have given up on telling me her really important information.

"Uh, Danielle?"

"Let them go first," she mumbled with an irritated frown, "so that I can at least tell you without disturbance."

CHAPTER TWELVE

The Questionable Object
(1)

"Wow, just…wow." Danielle grunted as Chima excitedly waved his nauseating snacks at our faces. Whatever they put inside that sausage roll agreed with its eventual destiny, and the so-called doughnut smelled like an expired mix of dough and sugar.

As if by magic, Chima and Olivia had brought us into the bakery's midst of famished children who were enamoured with the aroma and aesthetic of the pastries and were chowing down. The school's official baker, Mr. Kain Daniels, was, as far as I knew, by far the most professional artist in the world of baking. Where some people had the gift of drawing so well that it looked like a photograph and others could design the complex operations of a Boeing jet, this man could turn flour, water, and other elements into mouth-watering pastries. He's the only baker who has lasted more than a year in the school's employment and was one of its money-making sources; no matter how high he set the price of the snacks, students thronged there daily to satisfy their cravings. Even I was once under the spell of Mr. Kain and his wonderful creations. He was the only man I trusted enough to eat a fish roll from, but now, being anywhere close to delicacies reminded me of being in a toilet. A public toilet at that. It wasn't his fault, though; it was the constant nausea.

"You guys, he made hotdogs today!" Olivia squealed with pleasure, increasing the decibel by a few notches. Her excitement was infectious, and other students already there, admiring the assortment of snacks, beamed more at Olivia's announcement. Not Danielle; she rolled her eyes at Olivia and said dryly, "Thanks for making my ears bleed, Olivia. You just increased the headache I had been managing."

"Oh, you have a headache! That explains the sudden change in your attitude since Government class," Olivia said with obvious concern.

"Err, not really."

"I'm so sorry!" She looked crestfallen until Danielle confirmed that she wasn't angry. The mood lifted somewhat, and she allowed herself to make a joke.

"But guy," She tapped Olivia's chest and let out a light snort, "Your tie is practically gone."

"It's probably with Daniel." Chima chimed in. "Maybe you went to his house and did something, then you forgot it there."

Now that was a joke that got a rise of Olivia. She spread her palm and lashed a huge whack across Chima's back., yet all he did was laugh loudly because, as hard as she did, the slap bounced off him painlessly.

Chima then fanned her flames by firing off his usual insult to her: "Shortie."

I tuned out of their usual bickering, with Danielle now trying to break them off. I spotted Mr. Godwin in the distance, chatting with his best friends, Mr. Felix and Mr. Wale. He suddenly turned and noticed my tenacious stare at him, then proceeded to glare back at me with that same suspicious look.

"Uh Amanda?" I quickly broke our stare-off and faced Danielle, Olivia, and Chima, all shooting me strange looks.

"Uh, yeah?" I replied.

"What's up with you and..." Ah, I see. I had forgotten about how good they were at eye-tracking and didn't anticipate them ending their dispute that quickly.

"Oh that? Well...wait. Danielle," I paused, shifting the conversation towards anything that I wasn't the centre of. "You had something to tell us before Olivia and Chima kidnapped us from class."

"We didn't kidnap."

"Yes, you did." Danielle shot back before taking a deep breath.

"Yeah, ok, I do have something to tell you."

"You mway pwoceed!" We all starred at Chima in disgust and signalled for him to shut his mouth and to stop acting two-year-old.

"When I was collecting the Government note from Mr. Akpan's laptop, I noticed an oddly named file on his system. It was something called 'The IOR'."

"The IOR?" We chorused in confusion.

"Yup."

"How is that a suspicious file? It could be just part of his work or something else. You do know that he's not only a teacher, right?"

Olivia had a valid point. We did not know our teachers' private lives, so that file didn't seem to be of particular significance.

"I know that, obviously," Danielle retorted as she grabbed Olivia's bottle. "It didn't seem strange until I clicked the folder, and all I saw were four subfolders. Men, women, boys, and girls."

"Were you able to check any of them out?"

She shook her head in disappointment. "Nope. I was about to, but then Mr Akpan saw where I was and defensively snatched his laptop away from me. I heard him mutter, 'I hope she didn't see'."

We agreed that that did seem strange. Even if the files were completely harmless, his reaction to Danielle would suggest something more ominous.

Chima was the first to speak after we all ruminated on it for a short while. "I mean, that may seem weird, but it's not weird enough to be an issue. It is his laptop, after all. There are things I won't want anyone to see on mine." With that, he got up from the chair and headed back towards the pastries.

"He's right, though. He's oddly right." Danielle reasoned loudly and started off a few seconds after Chima. "Well, now I'm craving pastries too."

And with that, she was gone, leaving only Olivia and me on our bench. But we were not there for long; her attention drew towards her boyfriend, signalling her over.

"I'll be back!" She chanted cheerily as she sprinted off to meet him, and just like that, I was left with nothing but the noise and my thoughts. There is mostly noise at this point.

I began observing the crowd, which thankfully paid no attention to me, and I could safely watch people carry out their activities. They were mostly playful teenagers, and I tried to imagine what their own thoughts were as they played about. I also noticed that Mr. Godwin had exited the hall and heaved a sigh of relief. I didn't want to engage in disconcerting staring content anymore. All that was left to do was find out - 'I want you.'

'Amanda... I want you.'

"We're back!" I practically flew off my seat, bumping my head painfully into the tiles. I felt myself blacking out, and in that brief moment, I sighted two arms out-stretched towards me, followed by two concerned expressions and a lot of unnecessary background input.

"I thought the whole point of announcing our presence was to avoid things like this." Chima commented as they both lifted my prone body off the ground. I ended up shrugging off his support while a teacher came running towards us.

"Is she alright?" Fear dripped from her voice, and she instinctively placed her palm towards my forehead— not the part of my body that was not impacted, but I chose not to make any such corrections.

Not the place I almost destroyed, but I probably shouldn't say anything.

"She looks fine," she answered herself.

"She's fine jare! She's just an attention seeker." It wasn't surprising that one of the mean girls piped in. Miss Olabitan scowled at the group and eventually chased them out of the dining hall.

"But guy, what happened?" Chima still looked shaken, but I had no reply. I couldn't tell them that a certain person's voice chose to haunt me in a public place. My mind hadn't done that to me in a while, so even I was battling a lot of turmoil right now.

"You guys just scared me, that's all." Yeah, that's all. Let's not add to their individual issues, I told myself. Amanda, you're fine.

"SHORT BREAK IS OVER! EVERYONE TO YOUR CLASSES RIGHT NOW!"

"Noooo! I wanted more hotdogs!"

"Chima, get yourself together; he ain't dying! You'll see him tomorrow," Danielle told him laughingly.

Chima pouted and stomped towards the entrance, and we, his friends, gave him some distance so as to avoid being seen with this giant toddler. From the corner of my eyes, I caught sight of the same junior girl I saw the previous day.

The timing was impeccably eerie. It was the exact same scenario, just during a different day and a different break. The only difference was that I was now looking at her from my left, not my right, and it wasn't a teardrop that halted me in my steps. It was a scar. A fresh scar, one that resembled a permanent eyeliner.

That girl. Something told me that I needed to meet that girl.

"You guys!" Olivia's high-pitched voice ripped the attention I trained on the junior, bringing me back to the world that consisted of other people apart from myself and the girl.

"I found my tie!"

"No way." Danielle's sarcastic applause complimented Chima's overflowing laughter. I waited a bit for them to realise that Olivia didn't announce it with a smile.

She announced it in panic.

"Guys… I found my tie!" She repeated it with an even deeper frown.

"Isn't that good news?" Chima asked, confusion running around his features.

"Yeah, why are you frowning?"

She took a deep breath and began walking away from the dining hall. We shuffled after her.

"Olivia!" Chima called out, grasping Olivia's arm before she fainted out of panic.

"Girl, what is the matter?"

She turned around and stared at us, – eyes widening, her knees failing, and her arms shaking.

"I found my tie."

"Yes?!" We all chorused in anticipation. Well, Danielle and Chima chorused because I was silently awaiting the punchline.

"I found my tie with a divider."

"O…k?"

She took a deep breath before letting out some shocking words.

"I found my tie with a divider… that was covered in blood."

Part Three

CHAPTER THIRTEEN

The Questionable Object (2)

"She now told me that you had dropped Geography since, and you kept us in the dark! You didn't even deem it fit to consult with us before dropping it, abi? When you know your father also studied Geography!"

"Mummy," Diana began defensively, "I genuinely did not want to write Geography anymore."

"I don't understand o. When I was your age…" This is the perfect time to tune out my mother and sister's usual fiery disagreements.

These afternoon drives were deeply uncomfortable for me. It felt like I was driving down a steep, rocking slope—almost like being on a bullet train that had lost control and was hanging on just barely. Trying to maintain mental stability took a physical toll on me, and being trapped in the car with two volatile individuals left me careening. They both had strong, unyielding opinions on every subject under the sun, and neither was willing to concede any ground to the other. Listening to them alone was exhausting. To top it all off, I had an additional issue plaguing my mind. I couldn't fully conclude that this particular case was actually a case, but the possibility that it could be did a number on my already unstable mental state.

Earlier that day

"Covered in blood?" Danielle questioned with concern dripping through her voice. Olivia could only nod with shock glaringly displayed on her face. We glanced at one another quietly before the voices of angry teachers made us run and hide under the back stairwell.

I slumped down on the floor, fear and tiredness wrenching my nerves as I tried to process this unsettling turn of events.

"Do you think someone is… you know…" Chima whispered.

"Either that or someone was attacked with it."

I remained silent while my friends tried to develop a backstory.

"It's concerning either way." Olivia had finally stopped shaking, and she was measuring out her words heavily.

"Blood was on that divider," she continued. "Unless some psychotic lady had her period on that divider, it's clear that some skin cells were torn apart before the blood got to the object."

We thought about what Olivia said. She was right. Even if it wasn't a deliberate attempt, someone would have had to stick the divider into a body for the pointy end to be covered entirely in blood.

"But what if it was also just an accident, though?" Danielle's intuitive tone peaked as she challenged Olivia's words. "It could be that someone just had a serious accident with the divider and forgot about the divider when they ran out to get treated."

Olivia slumped down on the floor with me, her expression revealing the gears spinning in her head as she tried to reason out what Danielle said.

"Yes, that could be a possibility, but I highly doubt it."

"Why?"

She went on to explain how she had first found the divider on the chair and not on the table, which she thought was suspicious because if a student was working, it wouldn't have been on the chair. She went on to discount the possibility of a student using it, as it didn't hold any water, even among us three. But her next point made it clear that some malice was involved:

"I found the divider inside my tie," she stammered.

"Why didn't you say that before?!" Chima exclaimed, stomping around anxiously. Olivia sighed loudly, Danielle held her head in her palms, and I looked on numbly.

And then we realized a third possibility: an issue of self-harm. We were definitely aware of what it was and the severity of the problem, but we never thought that we would encounter such on this school grounds. It was a shock greater than that from an electric socket.

"Someone needs help." Olivia's voice broke the uneasy silence we had drowned ourselves in. Her shoulders rose as she assumed the posture of a troubled yet courageous soldier who became suddenly aware of a harsh reality but determined to overcome it. "We need to find out who the student is before it's too late."

"Wait o, why is that our problem though? We're all acting like we were appointed as the defenders of the school or something. We haven't even confirmed that it's self-harm."

She shrugged calmly, saying, "I would rather try than witness some future headlines about that student's death. We have to at least try and find out who the person is."

"I agree though," Danielle chimed in, fully supporting Olivia's argument, "We'll just sneakily find out who left the divider and ask why blood was on it. If it turns out to be nothing, then we can carry on with our lives."

"Hello? Who is down there?!" A loud female voice trilled down the stairs. "Whoever is there, head to your class now!"

Chima paused, looked at the rest of us girls, and said,

"We'll talk more later I guess." We nodded in agreement and quickly slipped through the first-floor back entrance before we got caught and received a vicious telling-off.

Present Time

"Amanda, do you not have a mouth to answer again?!" I was jolted back into the ride home with a glaring Diana and our agitated mother.

"Sorry mummy. I slept off."

"Slept off, ke? So, if you were in someone else's car, you would just sleep off and, God forbid—get kidnapped, abi?"

"No mummy." I made sure to bite my tongue hard so that no backtalk slipped through my mouth.

Throughout the rest of the ride, I made sure to appear present while I threw around random thoughts in my head. Eventually, I sighted the gate to the house in the distance, gleaming in the sunlight despite the paint starting to peel off. My parents chose to use barbed wires to ensure anyone who attempts to climb over faces ultimate death while we sleep safely and soundly. I've seen some people safeguard their houses with broken glass pieces instead of wires, which to me seemed like a brilliant way to recycle the overflowing waste our country generates by the ton every month.

"They should open the gate fast o." My mum began ranting to herself and honking even before we reached the gate. Diana mumbled under her breath, but I made out the words, 'You're too impatient' and 'You talk too much.' I decidedly avoided turning towards her because I knew the death stare that awaited me if I did. My mind never stopped focusing on the issue I was dealing with, but the discovery in school placed another layer on my already distressed mind.

Who could possibly be harming themselves in our school?

It might not have been confirmed that it was a self-harm case, but the possibility of it was never a question I thought I would have to think about. Life is truly unpredictable.

CHAPTER FOURTEEN

A Series of Confrontation

The principal's office. It is well-ventilated with a personalized mini-fridge stocked with assorted drinks and was the only room in the entire school that actually has a stable ceiling fan, as all the other fans were practically hanging by a thread. Each floor tile was scrubbed clean and polished to the point that it could be used as a mirror. The lighting could improve every photo quality on my smartphone, and the cushions were so plush that you could be persuaded to donate your legs forever.

I was able to glean all these observations due to the fact that on this uneventful Friday morning, I was compelled to sit through a meeting between my parents and Mr. Okoko. I deftly avoided the interrogative stare of my mother on my left side. My father, as always, was scrolling through his endless messages and missed phone calls with his usual stone-faced expression.

I anxiously glanced towards his antique clock as he cleared his throat before finding the perfect accent to use.

"Thank you for coming again, Mr. and Mrs. Ekhator."

"It is never a problem, sir." My mother represented both herself and my father, as he clearly wasn't mentally present for the meeting. Or he probably just did not care.

Mr. Okoko fished out a crimson folder from his wobbling stack of files and adjusted his glasses.

"We have had countless meetings to discuss Amanda's sudden behavioural changes. And I must say that the matter still persists." He flipped through the crimson fold, 'hmmming' at the flip of every page.

"She has still not resumed any of her club meetings. She continues to skip classes, and Miss Ogunnubi has especially reported her to me over and over."

I could feel my mum intensify her glare at me, but I just maintained eye contact with the folder to evade all the wordless interrogations her eyes were shooting at me. My dad lifted his head from his phone and asked the only question that mattered to him: "How are her grades?"

Mr. Okoko switched his attention from my folder to his laptop to give my dad the most recent version of the question.

"Well," he said. "Her C.A. took a downturn this term, but we have not yet had our mid-term examinations, so she can still make up for it. The examinations start two weeks from now, on the 13th of February."

At that, my dad levelled his eyes at me. I thought, 'Great. Now both sides are glaring straight at me'. The heat from their stares was enough to melt some of the chill I felt from being in this miniature North Pole of an office. Mr. Okoko must have had an extremely low tolerance for the Nigerian heat if the temperature in his office was this chilly and could turn my sweat into hail.

"You better pass your midterm exam." My dad grumbled to himself, but loudly enough for me to hear, instantly checking out of the discussion to continue tapping away on his phone.

The principal then turned back towards my folder and continued, "Ah yes. We've also gotten more reports from our school nurses that she has been vomiting, fainting, and apparently not eating enough meals to sustain her body."

"But she eats breakfast and dinner at home, abi, don't you?" My mum queried. I nodded quickly and forced a believable smile and a thumbs-up with both hands.

Mr. Okoko gently dropped my folder and leaned forward on his desk, his head lightly resting on his chin. "She may have some sort of eating disorder? Maybe she needs to get checked."

"My child cannot be ill; I forbid it!" My mum snapped impatiently. This was one of the issues our family constantly dealt with. My parents, mum in particular, refused to believe that their children could be attacked by any kind of disease, illness, or sickness. To them, everything can be solved through the power of prayer, which I agree with in principle, but I don't think it's wise to simply pray and not get treated when one's body is battling an illness. If a person gets stabbed in the knee with a knife, mere prayer will not magically remove the knife from the knee, nor would it magically heal the entire leg.

My mum began speaking in tongues, basically ending the entire conversation. The principal only added a caveat about how I was flirting with suspension if I didn't get my act together, but thankfully my parents were mentally checked out by this point.

"Well then, thank you for your time, Mr. and Mrs. Ekhator."

"My child cannot be sick; I cast out all demons that want to overtake my child. They will not stay."

"Uh mummy, the meeting is over." I knew she didn't hear me as the Holy Spirit had taken over her at that point, so I just informed my dad that I was heading back to class and made my way out of the office.

As soon as I swung the door open, Mr. Aloba's laptop nearly smacked me in the face.

"Sorry, dear, I'm waiting for the principal," he started to say.

The principal heard his voice and called him in. "You can come in!"

I made a way for him so he could enter the office without bumping into me or my parents. I was about to head off in the opposite direction of my parents when I felt a gush of wind fly right past me. I froze in confusion as I watched Mr. Aloba sprint down the hallway, his colleagues equally stunned by the sudden and weird take-off.

Mr. Okoko sat up in shock, not understanding what just happened. I saw that my mother was oblivious to the drama going on as she was still speaking in tongues, and my father...

Wait.

My dad looked enraged.

I understood that Mr. Aloba was unprofessional in his conduct, but whatever was left of my intuition told me that he was angry for a more personal reason. His fingers balled up into fists, and his knuckles turned ghostly white. It seemed like he grew a foot taller in his inexplicable anger, and veins stuck out from the sides of his neck. He spun around to approach Mr. Okoko, demanding to know if Mr. Aloba was a teacher at the school. "Is that man a teacher here?" Mr. Okoko tried to answer his question as politely as he could, while my mother immediately jumped in and tried to assuage her husband's temper.

"Honey, it's ok. Not here, not now."

"Can he answer my question first?!" His voice rose

with each word he spoke, his veins on the verge of exploding. If the atmosphere was awkward before, it is definitely tense now.

"Does he work here?!"

"He is one of our biology teachers," Mr. Okoko said in a subdued tone as he gestured towards the chair my dad previously occupied. "Please, sir, I do not understand where this anger came from, but I can assure you that I will deal with his reckless behaviour."

My dad cut him off and boomed. "Do you not keep track of your staff at all?!"

I tried to signal to Mr. Okoko that when my dad was angry, his ears basically stopped working. He was unable to process any words spoken towards him in that moment, as his mind would not comprehend anything apart from the next sentence he's going to use in his one-sided argument. He shouts, he yells, and he sometimes curses in his native tongue, then his anger settles for about a minute or two before it erupts all over again.

Simply put, there's no such thing as a conversation when my dad loses his temper.

"Do you know what that man did?!" My mum frantically began cautioning him in Edo. Whatever she was saying had taken away two veins from my dad's forehead already.

"Sir, if we could just calmly discuss what my employee has done to trigger your rage, I could offer my assistance in solving this issue." My dad finally took his seat, his body still visibly unstable. If not for my mother's powerful spirit and how she was able to take out the air from my dad's sail, Mr. Okoko would most likely be in a headlock in the middle of shattered glass and ripped-up folders.

Mr. Okoko eventually asked for me to leave his office so he could handle the matter without stirring further gossip within the school and so that my dad wouldn't transfer his volatile aggression to me. Luckily for him, I was too depressed to spread such news. And even if I wasn't, the entire school didn't have to know about my family's violent tendencies.

I safely exited his office and noiselessly shut his door, then decided to drag my weak body into the elevator and see where it took me while I pondered over my dad's absurd behaviour. Unfortunately for me, the unofficial tattler of the school, Miss Ogunnubi, shouted my name from across the corridor. She seemed unhinged in her unbalanced wig and her mismatched clothing.

"I hope the principal finally punished you because I cannot take this anymore." She waited impatiently for me to reach where she stood, but I had no energy to entertain her this morning.

"Amanda! You can see me waiting for you, and you are dragging your feet! I did not know you to be this disrespectful." I couldn't tell if she was angry or surprised at my defiance, but I didn't care. I just shrugged. The anger that clouded her face made it seem like she was about to begin her villain arc. I was already picturing which power she'd possess: her red pen would turn into some sort of flaming stick, and her glasses would most likely shoot infinite F's.

"You have a bright future! But you choose to ruin it with your actions." Oh, she was still talking.

Lord God, please send an angel to take her on some missionary journey towards the Maldives.

"Miss Ogunnubi, your attention is needed in JS2D." I leaned to my right and noticed a male security guard firmly holding his baton and patiently waiting for a response so he could unfreeze his legs. Miss Ogunnubi then looked angrily at me, groaned internally, and then mustered out a polite 'I'm on my way' before reluctantly leaving my sight.

Ah! God truly answers prayers.

"Someone should call Mr. Aloba to my office now!"

Upon hearing Mr. Okoko's angry demand, the staff below scurried towards the elevator and stairs. The receptionist began smashing random numbers into her phone, her fingers on the verge of snapping in half.

"You there! Go to your class!" Mrs. Adeola, the other receptionist who wasn't as panicked as Miss Sarah, instructed before all hell broke loose on this current floor. I nodded absentmindedly and resumed my journey towards the elevator. After reaching it and instantly being welcomed with its open arms, I dragged my feet into the elevator and punched any button.

"Please don't send me there!" My ears picked up Mr. Aloba's voice, and the door seemed to pick up on the mood as it began closing in slow motion. That gave me enough time to see his terrified, ghostly expression, his vibrating frame, and the violent clasp he had on his tie.

At least now I was certain of one thing.

My dad knows Mr. Aloba, and for the first time, it wasn't a friendship he ended up building with him.

CHAPTER FIFTEEN

The First Suspect

A slam. A zip. A clap. Then, a sigh.

"Ah! English was such a bore."

"I agree. All that man did was give essay after essay. Like, I sincerely wanted to stone him."

Danielle sniggered at Olivia's comment. I watched both of them in silence as I battled the fresh turmoil my mind had just been experienced.

My dad knows Mr. Aloba.

My dad hates Mr. Aloba.

"Everyone taking Further Maths should go to the Maths lab now! Mr. Adefolarin is waiting for you!" For some reason, one of the students thought it was necessary to yell out this announcement.

I heard Danielle and Olivia praise the Lord that it wasn't a compulsory subject. If it were, we all would currently be depressed. Even beyond depressed, because those formulas were definitely not normal. Well, in fairness, no formula is normal, but those formulas? With all the 'dy' and the 'dx' and questions that only contain letters, yet the answer would be expected in digits? No, thank you. I'll pass.

"Anyways sha, I want to sleep." Danielle then proceeded to fake a yawn, but Olivia punched her so hard that even my insides felt the impact.

"Ahn ahn! What is your problem?"

"Shebi you have forgotten what we promised to find out?"

"What thi— Ohhh! Ah, I've even forgotten sef. Ehn, that didn't mean you should now punch me na." She hissed at Danielle's comment and turned to face me instead, awaiting my reply to her lingering suggestion. I just did what I always did to most people's questions.

Shrug.

She took my neutral reaction as a yes and signalled for all three of us to pack our belongings and head towards one of the abandoned classrooms. We would've waited for Chima, but he had silently slipped out of the classroom to 'settle the beef' he had with his Commerce teacher, Mr. Aluko.

Since my bag was practically empty, I patiently waited for Olivia to completely stuff all her useful and useless school items, especially her entire make-up kit, into her newly-bought neon backpack. Danielle was thankfully more organized, as her belongings had all been packed according to size, alphabet, and level of importance. She was also waiting for Olivia to finish smooshing her things into one another so they could all fit in her bag, but she definitely wasn't patient with it.

"You're the one that said we should go, yet you're the last person to get ready."

"Don't mind her! Olivia is always slow." Eniola, the second beauty guru of the class, laughed while popping gum in her mouth. Olivia and Danielle were friendly with her, but I wasn't. Even before I entered this depressive state, simply because there was never a need to. The reason Olivia and I became friends in the first place was because, to everyone's surprise, she was a part of the debate team that I used to participate in. In Danielle's case, she loved sports and I used to; so we bonded due to similar sporting injuries and mutual complaints about the coach's inhumane workouts.

That was until, you know what.

"Eniola, just shut up." That just made her laugh harder, and Danielle joined them in the heartwarming moment. Unlike them, I couldn't find humour in anything, so I just withdrew into my self-deprecating thoughts.

"Abeg please, face your front ode. Amanda ooo, let us be going!"

"And where are you off to?" Justin, the TikTok king, queried Olivia.

"How is that your business?" He just shot her his

signature smirk which almost all the girls fell for.

Too bad for him; Olivia was already taken.

"Abeg! Amanda, Danielle, let's be going! Stupid boy." He chuckled lightly at Olivia's insults, winked at Danielle, and completely ignored my presence.

Didn't bother me though. He wasn't all that anyway.

We were finally in the hallway which was a strange mixture of peace and clamour - not a surprise considering that it was only the senior school that was on this floor, and our set was the smallest out of them all. Other sets reached up to more than half of a hundred, while ours was only around half of that.

"By the way, Amanda." Danielle halted her steps as Olivia called the elevator.

"Mmm?"

"How did your meeting with Mr. Okoko and your parents go?"

"Oh yeah, that." Alright. Now is the time to make the ultimate choice:

Option A: Tell them everything just went meh.

Option B: Shrug as usual.

Option C: Narrate the entire story of how Mr. Aloba and my dad appeared to have some sort of history that definitely wasn't pleasant, and that it was an issue I took as being in dire need of solving.

What to pick?

"It went meh." It came out almost automatically.

"So, no new punishment?" Danielle asked, apparently unconvinced by my first answer.

"Nope." They didn't need to know all that. It was a family matter, one I had to handle by myself.

Yet Danielle went on. "You do know that the science class had Biology, and Mr. Aloba was furiously called to the principal's office when you were still in there, right?" Shoot, I thought. What now?

"So, if you weren't punished, why was he called there?" The elevator lightly pinged, and out stepped Simi and Joshua, giggling.

"Weren't you guys fighting like, throughout this week?" Olivia questioned.

"Love is love, abeg." Simi beamed proudly.

"Sha don't let the teachers see you." Simi waved us off and dragged Joshua along with her down the hallway. Danielle scoffed, "Wahala o."

Discarding the distraction, we finally got on the elevator.

"Oya. What happened?" She resumed interrogating me.

Should I really tell them? What if I tell them about this issue and accidentally blurt out my other issues? No. I cannot have them pity me.

"Nothing really. Just that he forgot to print out some

important documents, I guess. Nothing relating to my parents or me."

They nodded.

That's good, they bought it.

"Well, anyway, regarding the divider issue, we should start narrowing down who we think might be, well, you know."

"I don't think it's a junior," Danielle commented while casually looking at her reflection on the elevator walls. "I don't think they even know what self-harm is yet."

That comment didn't settle well with me. My mind immediately flew to the girl who had something similar to scar marks beside her eyes.

"What if it is a junior, though?" I pitched in, gaining their attention instantly.

"Why do you think so?"

"Well…"

I highlighted the two moments I had seen that junior. The first time I saw a tear, the second time I saw a scar.

"But why would someone harm themselves beside their eye? It doesn't even make sense."

Olivia derailed Danielle's train of thought. "It's actually very possible. But I don't think her issue would be a self-harm case."

"But she's definitely going through something." I

retorted calmly while leaning against the wall, "I'm really curious where she got that scar from. It doesn't seem natural."

Danielle stared at me in silence, but Olivia quickly pitched in.

"We could just keep an eye out for the girl just in case. Do you even know who she is?"

"Eh," I muttered to myself as I tried to draw out any distinctive quality the girl had. The only standout feature I could remember was, "She had an incredibly neat bun."

They both gaped at me.

"Really? That's all you can-" Olivia started.

"Wait o, calm. How neat was the bun?" Danielle's curiosity raced.

Olivia just hissed and rolled her eyes while I responded calmly.

"Neater than most buns."

"Don't tell me." Danielle's expression suddenly fell, worry and confusion spreading over her face. Olivia too seemed confused, and she began to tap Danielle's arms, demanding answers that none of us had.

"It's most seniors who pack their hair in a bun. The juniors usually just let their hair fall down, but there's one particular junior whose hair alone would pass her off as a senior because it's her sister that does her hair."

"Ehen? I've seen like over ten juniors with buns."

Danielle shook her head aggressively. "I know! But like she described her bun as incredibly neat, and there's only one junior who has an incredibly neat bun."

"Who? Ohhh! Is it not… Ahhhh!" Olivia stumbled back in shock. They both eventually stared at me, waiting for me to express my own shock. In that split second, I realized that I knew who the girl was.

"So, you're telling us that Cynthia's sister is the junior?"

Yes. The girl who was crying and had a strange but very fresh scar beside her eyes was the sibling of an old friend of ours.

A friend none of us certainly planned to speak to ever again.

CHAPTER SIXTEEN

It's Actually an Issue

"Cynthia's sister ke?!" Chima exclaimed. His jolt caused his plantain chips to fly out of the packet and join the litter on the floor.

"Yes, "We all collectively sighed before Chima asked another question.

"Are you sure we're talking about the same Cynthia?" Olivia nodded in affirmation, yet he didn't want to accept it.

I mean, generally, no one wanted to accept that Cynthia's sister—the sibling of the girl we had all once been best buds with—was already thinking about ending her life. Okay, maybe not ending her life, but she was surely facing something that led to that prominent scar beside her eye. Something deep down just told me that it wasn't a natural part of her face. If it was, well, you learn new things every day.

"That means we all have to talk to Cynthia."

"Excluding me." I quickly removed myself from that future confrontation. There was no way I was going to have a conversation with someone I had thrown up all over. After that vomiting incident, she distanced herself from all of us because she thought I was becoming a negative influence on her and deemed the rest crazy for still hanging out with me.

"I exclude myself too o!" Olivia shook her head, "I don't want that girl's trouble."

After noticing that Danielle also supported Olivia and I's collective decision to not converse with Cynthia, Chima reluctantly sighed and decided to brainstorm a new plan.

"Ok, then, since none of you want to speak with her, I would question her myself."

"Are you insane?"

"See, we have to at least ask if she's aware that her sister might be going through something. It's her sister after all."

Danielle groaned in agreement. "For once, Chima is right."

"For once?!"

"Don't let us start." Chima just grumbled and furiously dumped all the chip crumbs into his mouth.

Danielle ignored Chima and carefully explained how we would still need to speak with Cynthia eventually. If her sister was suffering and we suspected something, we couldn't keep her in the dark about it, despite the recent turn of events. It made sense to inform Cynthia about it, but it didn't mean actually speaking to her would be an easy task.

Cynthia was a fully fledged science-oriented girl who had a reputation for holding outstanding grudges against people. Even if all you did was step on her shoe, she would harbour a deep resentment against you for weeks and months without necessarily expressing it; except if you fell on your knees to scrub off the tiny speck of dirt. It didn't mean she was a bad person, but one needed to know how to confront her about her attitude.

Unfortunately, in my case, our friendship ended because I stopped being concerned about anything else in my life aside from my personal issue, and the incident took place during the first week of the commencement of the abuse. It was a phase I hadn't become accustomed to as much as I was now, so I cut everything and everyone around me off. As a result, I didn't know how to go back to her or apologize for the way I embarrassed her in broad daylight, and our friendship died a sudden death. I remembered indirectly apologizing to her in the moment, but that must have sounded insincere since I never brought it up again. This was how I lost a majority of my friends—by taking no accountability for any hurt I caused them. I was just humbly thankful that I had this stubborn trio who didn't give up on me, no matter how I seemed to behave.

"So Chima, you'll be the one to talk to her." Danielle concluded, and Chima silently nodded.

The siren blared at that moment, muting all the rest of Olivia's statement and causing the pair of Danielle and Chima to laugh. I, on the other hand, remained stone-faced.

"We didn't hear you o."

"Whatever. Thank God it's lunch time sha. Oya Amanda, let's go."

I leaned back into the wooden chair and said, "I'm not going today. Still feeling nauseous."

"Awww, I wanted your meat." I could see Danielle readying to once again lash her Chima for his gluttony. Olivia was already skipping towards the door.

"Wait for us nau!"

Chima didn't slow down as he said, "Then hurry up! Amanda, we'll see you later." I gave him a thumbs-up as they all rushed out of the door to grab some food.

In their absence, I began to think about things on my own. I knew that I would have to speak to Cynthia again sometimes in the distant future, but I didn't know it would have to be because her sister could potentially be putting herself in danger. We were in separate classes and had separate groups of friends, so if this issue hadn't come up, we might have gone a year without needing to speak to each other.

It seems like life does have its ways to make people talk, no matter what.

As the silence grew, my vision suddenly began to blur, and a blinding headache hit my head with full force. I positioned my head on the rough desk and began to cry. The tears never gave me notice before they rushed out of my eyes whenever they had a chance to. With the volume of tears I'd shed in recent weeks, it was surprising that I had not run out of tears yet. So they kept coming.

It was now time to deeply think about the issues around me, but my fingers brushed against a piece of paper beneath my desk, and that interrupted the flow of my painful thoughts.

"What is this sef?" I asked myself as I tried to fish the paper out. When I did, I slowly began uncrumpling it purely out of curiosity, just to see if it had some sort of value or if I had the green light to discard it.

Well, the contents certainly had value, alright.

"I don't know what to do. My mum is a part of the I.O.R., and she threatens to beat me up if I report her. I hate having her as my mother. She knows exactly what she's doing to people, yet she doesn't care. I don't even know if my dad is aware of what she's doing, but I just want to escape this house before she does something to me too. I now know why she doesn't want me to become a boarder, she's probably plotting something against me already. I don't feel safe at home. Please let my graduation date comes soon; I can't take this anymore."

Hmm.

The I.O.R.

Those three letters struck a chord in me. They sounded familiar, as if I had previously heard them in some sort of conversation.

Ah, yes! Danielle mentioned something about those three letters. Specifically linked to Mr...

Flashback

"When I was collecting the Government note from Mr. Akpan's laptop, I noticed an oddly-named file on his system. It was something called 'The IOR.'"

"It didn't seem strange until I clicked the folder, and all I saw were four subfolders. Men, women, boys, and girls."

"I was about to check, but then Mr. Akpan saw where I was and defensively snatched his laptop away from me. I heard him mutter 'I hope she didn't see.'"

Present

"Mr. Akpan… he's involved in this I.O.R. stuff. And according to this abandoned letter (or essay or whatever English piece this is called), it wasn't just some personal computer file. It was something much bigger and more complicated than we all made it out to be. That's probably why we didn't deem it an actual issue to dwell on, but it seems like we should've.

Thankfully, this was something I could actually communicate to them, considering Danielle probably has more information about this I.O.R. but might have shrugged it aside, thinking it was no big deal.

"I should keep this." I neatly folded the vital piece of information and stuffed it into my tie. I said a silent prayer that the person who wrote it was safe, because it clearly sounded like they were in need of help.

There were many people in need of help. And it seemed like we were discovering them one after the other. Who knows, maybe someone will end up discovering mine someday.

But till then, it's best I stay quiet.

CHAPTER SEVENTEEN

Just Had to Run Into Each Other

Once again, I had holed myself up in the bathroom, sobbing, nearly ripping my braids out, and almost losing consciousness. It was a routine—a painful one at that. Whatever unknown miracle was preserving my internal organs from shutting down completely was one I would definitely refer to in the future. But as of now, all I could do was hope that that miracle would sustain me until my graduation day.

As I cross-checked that my body was in a more stable state, I carefully leaned my back against the toilet seat and allowed myself to breathe for a couple of minutes. Even though the toilet wasn't the best place to receive 'a breath of fresh air', the meaning at this precise time was more figurative than literal. Every second felt like I was going to pass out, and I felt it was increasingly approaching. I ended up closing my eyes to gain more stability, but a certain voice refused to give my mind even a second of peace.

'Don't forget that you're mine, love.'

I don't want to be yours. I really don't want to be yours, you sick pervert!

"Oh God! It's like the person has died inside there because they are not moving. Hello? Are you done?!" Someone aggressively banged on the toilet door, ostensibly offended that I had been there for this long, so I flushed the toilet in order to prove that I actually needed to be in there and not just occupying the space at the detriment of others.

"Coming out right now." I mumbled, mindlessly swinging the door open and almost slamming the hapless girl with it. She side-stepped it smartly before I got out, but if she were just a few inches closer, her face would definitely have received the full impact of the wooden door.

She made sure that I had completely exited the toilet before she slipped in, muttering words like "weirdo," thinking I couldn't hear her. It amazed me how people convinced themselves that saying things under their breath meant that they couldn't be heard at all. I might have been going through things, but I certainly was not deaf.

Clocking back into reality, I proceeded to splash water all over my face. An incredibly petrifying smell hit my nostrils with immediate effect, reminding me that I was truly in the ladies' bathroom. It seemed my frightening visions had temporarily muted my sense of smell. But it hit me with full force now, and I understood why the cleaners appeared to prefer the boy's toilets to the girls': the stink of used pads was choking.

I was just about to escape this literal dumpsite, but those plans were violently interrupted by a specific person I had wished, hoped, and prayed to never speak to for the rest of my years in this school. It was a tall order, given that we were on the same floor, in neighbouring classrooms, but in the same set.

Her voice preceded her entry. "They need to buy a much better air freshener, jeez!" And there she was. The girl that only Chima was supposed to confront, yet somehow, I was the one that had the misfortune of bumping into her, only moments after that revealing conversation.

For some reason, my legs suddenly developed a mind of their own and chose this time to refuse to move. I stood there awkwardly, watching her rinse, cleanse, and dry both her palms and face. As I struggled to command my legs to resume their normal function, the girl shrieked loudly and began blinking so fast that it seemed like her eyes had just learned how to open and close.

"Something's entered my eye, God!" She then frantically gestured towards me, beckoning me over to her side. "Blow my eyes right now!"

"What?"

"Blow my eyes jor!"

I'm not sure she knew who she was addressing, but the lingering humanity within me moved me to inhale and blow into her pupils. Hopefully her eyes can't sense bad breath, because if they could, hers might rip apart.

She soon resumed control of her eyes, and after blinking a few more times, she rubbed her eyes briefly, then opened both her eyes to ensure she could still see, and then took a disgusted step back when she realized who she had just communicated with.

"Oh, it's you. Urgh, it's you!" She scrunched up her nose and glided past my stationary self, smoothly ripping off a bit of the toilet roll positioned right beside the sink. A loud flushing sound—terribly increasing the disastrous smell in the bathroom—took over our tense interaction, and out came the girl I almost hit in the face with the toilet door. She stretched and yawned, and then waved at Cynthia before sneering at me.

Cynthia waved back lightly, then turned back to intensely glare at me. I even had to step back in confusion because of the intensity of her stare. It was as if she was pushing me towards the ground with her eyes; those eyes held a lot of unspoken words, most of which I presumed were curses.

She didn't remain speechless for long, and her verbalized words mirrored what I suspected she had in mind: "You know, I have a lot to say, but you're somehow just not worth it." A little scoff followed that statement. I leaned flatly into the wall close to the exit, planning to slip out from under her in a flash.

"You're just messed up," she continued. "It shows. It really shows."

"Abi o! I agree with you." I didn't realize we had company, so I looked to my right and saw the outsider shaking off the wetness in her palms. She egged Cynthia with countless thumbs ups, letting her know that she supported all the verbal blows she was aiming at me, and then she sauntered off towards the exit.

"Anyway, Cynthia, when you're done with her, we have extra chemistry classes after school." And with that, poof! She was gone.

I turned around to leave as well, but Cynthia seemed to think that now was the perfect time to confront me. Ironic, because I was supposed to be confronting her.

Well, not me exactly, but I was with my friends when they decided we had to say something. Still, I didn't envisage this encounter when I already had my own grave issues to contend with. Mine was equally as dire and needed a solution, lest the word "suicide" be intrinsically linked with our school.

However, Cynthia wasn't done with her tongue-lashing. "Next time, be less selfish, and maybe your currently messed up life won't be so messed up."

It seemed like that was the end of our discussion as

she walked out of the girls' toilet. I maintained my position: head hung low, back against the wall, eyes burning with tears. After she stepped out and the door swung shut, I bit hard on my lip and tried to prevent the tears stinging my eyes from falling down. But try as much as I did, I didn't know when I began to cry. Eventually, I calmed down (again), and when I pushed the door open, I nearly hit the incoming girls (again).

"Ahan!" they yelled. "You want to hit us abi?"

This time I was past caring, and I murmured, "Whatever."

I stepped out of the way and rushed out of their sight before the usual muttering began. I was already halfway down the corridor before my legs stopped jogging. Thankfully, the hallway I was strolling down was deserted, allowing me to glide down the walkway without interruption. I continued to contemplate everything around me. I wished I could exclude Cynthia's comments from my mind as well, but her sister being our suspect made it difficult to severe mental ties with her.

I had a feeling that the siren would soon start to sound, signalling the end of class and my opportunity to finally share the tie-protected secret with the rest of the class. Something told me that Olivia especially would urge us all to seek out the student who had carelessly left his or her heartfelt note underneath a random table.

"Hey, isn't that your sister?" I looked up, instantly making eye contact with Diana and Jessica—the only girl out of all her friends that she's known since when they were both in pre-kindergarten.

Their presence also made me realize that I had just strolled towards the SS3 department, and was currently parallel to SS3 S1, indicating the first science classroom in SS3. Their set was quite large in number, and the school had to build ten extra classrooms to comfortably accommodate future large sets without having overpopulated classrooms. But considering the vast number of extra classrooms on the top floor, the school authority clearly overdid it.

Diana just stared, shrugged, turned, and made her way far away from me. That was no surprise to me because it was her regular reaction any time we ran into each other in school, which wasn't frequent because of the distance between our classrooms. She also didn't usually go outside of her block for breaks, so unless she was reluctantly searching for me at closing time, we almost never saw each other in school.

Jessica, on the other hand, was evidently confused by the awkward interaction (or lack thereof) between us siblings and stood looking from one person to the other. It was weird to her that Diana turned away, and I didn't approach either. I half-expected Jessica to be aware of our frosty relationship, but it occurred to me that Diana didn't even deem me fit to be the subject of gossip with her friends. Not that I was complaining, though.

Jessica struggled to end the awkwardness and sputtered, "Uh, ok then. Take care, Amanda." Her apparent pleasantness caught me off guard. The fact that my sister couldn't stand me didn't mean that her friends were total b----es who didn't have any iota of decency in them. Jessica was still nice to me; no, we didn't hang out, but she was never hostile towards me.

Can't say the same for my sister, though. She had probably envisioned my head on a stake. Multiple times, for that matter.

CHAPTER EIGHTEEN

Stacks and Stacks of Problems

She couldn't stop pacing. Even after they had already shouted her name across various hallways, announcing that her dad was here to pick her up, and sent more than five people to pull her out of the classroom, her movements never slowed, and she never acknowledged any of them. Her eyes and mind were set on what she was reading—the piece of paper in her palms that contained concrete evidence that there was something disastrously wrong with the inner workings of our school.

Danielle was now thoroughly examining that paper—the secret that my tie had been tightly shielding.

"I just knew there was something off about those letters!" She finally spoke without breaking eye contact with the indirect S.O.S. message the person had written.

"Like... ah, I knew it!" It seemed to bug her that she ever discarded this issue in the first place. But even if we hadn't thrown it off, that paper was a clear indication that there was something absurdly wrong with those

175

three otherwise ordinary letters. Thank God, my name didn't contain any of them.

I continued waiting for Danielle to calm her down, before approaching her and gesturing towards the wall clock in our empty classroom.

"It's 4:10 p.m. Your dad will be upset by now."

"That's his business; this is way more important," she waved it off. "Besides, when have I ever been eager to go home?" True that. 'Home' isn't exactly the right word to describe how she felt about her family. It was not how I felt about my family, either.

"Anyways, now that it's confirmed that Mr. Akpan is linked to some sketchy letters, I finally have the go-ahead to sneak through his laptop. There are a lot of notes. I'll be collecting from him this term," she said mischievously. I wished Chima and Olivia were here so I could get their reactions to the strange note as well, but I had forgotten that it was a Friday and they were both involved in the same club: debating.

Anyone who knew them both would have safely guessed that, given their reputation for constantly bicker-ing.

"And I even had Government today. Ah, I wish I knew!"

I sighed, then took a seat to steady myself. "At least now we can expose that secret. And possibly help whoever wrote the note."

Danielle nodded in agreement, her fingers tightly gripping the note and threatening to rip it to shreds. We allowed silence to take over for a few minutes before a quiet knock caught our attention.

"Come in," she said. A junior boy stepped in cautiously, stopping right after his first step. His perfectly aligned tie was enough to tell me that he was a new student; no boy I had seen in this entire school cared what position their tie was facing, and even if they did face it straight, it would dance its way to another direction in less than five minutes. That's how unruly boys were. This one kept looking down at his feet, shuffling against them shyly as he debated passing on the message that brought him to our classroom.

"What is it?" Danielle fired at him strictly. She was usually calm and collected, but the paper she had in her palms had triggered a lot of rage in just a short period of time.

"I… um… the security said I should tell Danielle that her daddy is waiting for her," he stammered.

"I have heard. Oya bye-bye." She furiously waved the boy off and shifted her attention back to the paper.

"Danielle now," I lightly called. "Your dad will literally kill you if you keep delaying him."

She let out a disapproving sigh, then grabbed her bag from her chair, roughly swinging it over her shoulder.

"He can try. But anyway, we have to properly discuss

this. Would you be able to text this weekend?"

I also grabbed my lightweight bag while replying, "Um, definitely not at night, but I'm not really an online person anymore generally."

"Is there any time in the afternoon where you can be available for at least an hour?"

I shrugged and said, "I'll let you know if I'm available for a chat or call."

By now, I was practically pushing her out of the door. "Danielle! Did you not hear that you're going home?! Your dad has been waiting since!" She simply rolled her eyes, then waved goodbye before she trotted towards the fate that awaited her in the car.

I glanced at my watch, remembering that Diana also had club activities; which meant I was going to be aimlessly hanging out with my thoughts for quite some time. With that unfortunate realization on my mind, I headed towards the elevator to hide my next breakdown, mindlessly hitting the up arrow and leaning against the wall. The thoughts swarmed in immediately.

"Can't wait to taste you tonight, baby."

Leave me alone!

JUST LEAVE ME ALONE!

"Amanda." Mr. Adebayo's stern expression unglued me from the wall, but my fright instantly turned into suspicion as I noticed Miss Funmilayo standing behind him while deftly cradling stacks of files. Her height had doubled due to the wedges she wore, and her wig could-n't be more obvious.

But she wasn't the main cause of my suspicion. It was the man who was stylishly fleeing the scene that caused sirens to go off in my head.

"Good afternoon, Mr. Adebayo, Miss Funmilayo, and Mr. Aloba."

Upon hearing my greeting, he stopped speed-walking and turned around with fear written all over his face. His eyebrows furrowed, his grip tightened on his textbooks, and sweat slowly began forming on his forehead.

"Where are you going during this hour?" Mr. Adebayo questioned me, forcing my attention back towards him.

"I forgot something upstairs, sir."

"Is that so?" He kept staring at me, expecting further responses, but my gaze had diverted back towards Mr. Aloba who was stylishly trying to make a sneaky disap-pearance.

"Mr. Aloba." I began, dragging his attention back to me again. Mr. Adebayo tried to command my attention by constantly snapping his fingers and muttering how rude I was for discarding his presence that easily. But I had questions that urgently needed answers, and the only person who could answer them was not him.

"Mr. Aloba, do you know my dad?"

His eyes shot wide open. I already figured out that

they had some unpleasant connection, but seeing him react directly to my words removed any bit of doubt I may have had in my mind. He shuffled, re-adjusted his tie, clutched his books even tighter, and struggled to give a reply as he pursed like a fish caught in a hook.

Mr. Adebayo and Miss Funmilayo instantly glanced towards him with worrisome looks, as if they were pleading for him to not reveal the true answer to my persistent question. That was enough to tell me that they also knew the situation I was yet to identify, and there was a secret they were desperately trying to hide from me, which related to my dad somehow.

The air remained still as my question hung in the air, demanding an answer. Not just any one—an answer plausible enough to push me off the subject.

"Well, I…" He tried forcing out a reply, but Miss Funmilayo quickly intervened.

"Why won't we teachers have your parents' contacts? How do you think we reach them?"

I simply shrugged at her and replied, "I am aware of that, ma, but I'm asking for an entirely different reason."

"And that shouldn't concern you. You're supposed to be going, aren't you a day student?" Miss Funmilayo was mounting a sturdy defence right now, and I could tell that Mr. Aloba was grateful I didn't catch him alone. It was frustrating trying to get all my answers when he had his personal bodyguards shooing me away with their authoritative stances. I didn't even know all three of them were that close, considering Miss Funmilayo had just joined our school, and from previous observations, Mr. Adebayo and Mr. Aloba weren't ever close.

Mr. Adebayo then signalled to Mr. Aloba to keep moving, hinting that he shouldn't be frightened of a mere student who had nothing on him. I wanted to shout for him to come back and tell me what the deal was with him and my father, but he had already scurried to the left and disappeared from sight. Miss Funmilayo then pointed at the elevator, instructing me to go downstairs and wait in the lobby for my parents.

"Ok ma." I felt an anger surge across me, but I knew I couldn't act on that reckless emotion. Not with everything going on.

They both eventually left, hurriedly walking in the direction that Mr. Aloba had dived into. It took me all my strength not to run after them and demand the well-deserved explanations I wanted. How I wish I had found him alone and could persistently squeeze out all the answers from him without external interference. I would have crossed out this problem by now if not for those new besties of his.

After glaring at their retreating figures for a while, I debated continuing my journey into the elevator, but I had already forgotten the real reason I was making my way upstairs. Feeling slightly defeated, I headed back towards my classroom to sort out my thoughts, and it was about then that I saw a security guard frantically waving at me and shouting the words, 'You're going home!'

Home. Such an interesting theory. I wouldn't call my family house a home, as various people had ruined that word for me, but at least now I had countless missions in mind that would keep it occupied rather than it always having only one direction of thought.

My mind usually drifted off to what was awaiting me during the night. It had been two months since the first time, and it was now a routine I was used to. But by couching my problems in those of other people, I gave myself leeway to look forward to getting home. I didn't know it for sure, but I suspected that I would solve the mystery.

Typical Night Routine

Night time once again. He had already finished ravaging my body and was swiftly buckling his belt. His body was drenched in sweat; his muscles looked taut but grossly satisfied, and the smirk on his face only grew wider as he watched me gasp for air while quivering on the icy floor tiles.

"It gets sweeter with each passing day," he commented as he finally slipped on his shirt and cracked his knuckles. I kept my eyes down, fighting back the emotions my eyes threatened to leak while grasping my stomach in agony. The turmoil that punctured my insides was too great for my mind to absorb, and pain struck me from every direction of my body, even parts I had yet to identify.

I glanced towards my nightdress that he had thrown across the room and slowly began wiggling on the floor in an attempt to retrieve my clothing.

"Leave it." He commanded, hovering over me and

blocking my view of my dress. "You can take it when I'm gone. Right now, I'm still craving your body. No matter how many times we do this, it's just never enough."

I scooted backwards instinctively, hitting my back against my bedside and praying he didn't want to go on further this night. He continued staring at me intensely, grunting with pleasure and taking in the sight of my exposed body parts before eventually groaning and quietly exiting my room. I spat curses at the door after he left, but bit my lip to restrain myself from crying out loudly.

Eventually I did cry, and it took a while for me to stop crying and set out to retrieve my nightdress—a dazzling blue-patterned garment that sparkled under the dim light flowing in through the window. I wiggled and rolled as best as I could before I got close enough to snatch it. Some dust had settled on it by the time I retrieved it, and the fabric was icy cold instead of the warmth and comfort a pyjamas is supposed to provide.

I tried to pluck every speck of dirt off but ended up dusting it perfunctorily. Then I slipped it on, heard the dull vibration of my phone on my desk, and saw the light cut through the darkness. Typically, I would ignore it, but as I was already close to the window, I figured there was no reason for me not to distract myself with the phone, because right now, all my mind processed was the hammering pain in my abdomen and groin.

It must have taken about thirty minutes of scooting, wiggling, and tumbling, but I finally was able to lean against my desk, panting from both the pain and exhaustion. I felt around my table in search of the phone but experienced some sharp pain in the process. I found it and squinted through the blinding light emanating from the phone. Ironic, because it is currently set to the lowest level.

I scrolled through the pointless email ads, game notifications, and Snapchat friend suggestions- basically all the notifications that made people overestimate their importance in other people's lives, before getting to the WhatsApp notifications.

'5 missed calls from Olive. 00:06 a.m'

This girl. She knew that I didn't answer calls later than 7 p.m. each day. The most I could do was respond by messaging, and that's when my phone was with me in the wee hours of the morning after the man had finished his usual work- like right now. But today, all I could do was sigh and switch off my phone screen, then melt into the ground, wishing it could swallow me completely.

I remained paralyzed on the floor until more vibrations disturbed the quietness. I glanced towards my phone again and noticed Olivia's middle finger pointing at me. It was her profile picture that she was proud to show off wherever she went. I glared at the noisy device and ended up silencing her calls, but the light betrayed me every single time: despite being low, the darkness seemed to amplify the glare with each call she tried placing through. There was a simple solution to this though: I could just turn the thing entirely off, but the damage was done already: simply seeing one of Olivia's calls makes you increasingly curious why she's firstly up by 12:00 midnight, and secondly,, why she's calling you at that particular time instead of scrolling through TikTok. I gave up and answered the phone.

Olivia: *Finally, you picked up! I thought I would have to call you like fifteen more times!*

I rolled my eyes at her annoying persistence, but I didn't reply with anything more than a reluctant grunt.

Olivia: *Okay, I know I disturbed your night time peace or whatever, but I wanted to quickly call and tell you that Chima spoke to Cynthia today! Oh well, yesterday, but you get sha.*
Me: *Really?*
Olivia: *Yes o! Ah wait, what happened? You sound so sick over the phone.*

She picked up on the strain in my voice. Not surprising.

Me: *Vomit, but sha, what happened?*

Olivia: *Oya, don't be talking much, girl, lemme just fill you in quickly. So basically, we saw her on our way out of Debate Club, and I quickly left because me, I don't want problem. But then, when Chima came back to me, he said she said we should mind our own business, and that her sister was fine. I said okay ooo, me sha I will still meet the sister and ask her what happened.*

Me: *Hmm...*

Olivia: *But sha I'm talking to the sister next week, maybe Tuesday. That Cynthia girl is so blind, people can never realize the pain of people that they are literally living with. Chai, I cannot imagine.*

It felt like she was indirectly calling out my family right now. Yes, I knew she couldn't have been, but those words couldn't be more relatable to my current conundrum. It's so twisted how a lot of things can take place under someone's roof, yet everyone is so preoccupied with their lives that they never sense the pain of the person right beside them. It was a common issue, for sure, but I ticked my family's name into that category.

Me: *Hmm...*

*Olivia: Oya I've said all I want to say. Take care sha!
Don't throw up too much o. Bye girl.*

And just like that, call over. I set my phone down and accidentally moved my body carelessly, causing a different type of pain to shoot through my whole lower body. I slapped my hands over my mouth and screamed into my muffled palm. Clearly, I should have stayed in bed instead of moving around as much as I did this night. Now, I could barely walk back to the bed, let alone climb into it and fold myself into a position that wouldn't spook my mother if she found me in it.

I silently gazed at my bed as tears streamed down my face, but then suddenly, a heavy pounding on my door shook me to my core.

Please don't be her.

Being near the toilet, I spent all the rest of my willpower to scoot into the cubicle-sized bathroom. I heard the door click open and close, followed by slack footsteps. After a few seconds, I heard the door click back in place, and silence filled my room once again. I wanted to ponder who the second nightly visitor was tonight, but the soreness in my legs distracted me from giving it sufficient thought.

I wasn't prepared to go back into my room, though. Just being in the toilet had triggered a rush of vomit from within my belly, and it came rushing out with immediate effect. I positioned myself over the toilet bowl, grasped my braids above my head, and began to let it go. The process drained more energy out of me after being assaulted, and now I had to push through the burns in my throat and chest along with the pains in my lower region.

Thanks a lot, life.

CHAPTER TWENTY

An Unexpected Reveal

I dipped the mop back into the bucket and nonchalantly began to wipe the floor with the soapy, shaggy locks. Water splashed all over my crocs and surviving pair of joggers, indirectly cleansing me as I hadn't had my bath and refused to enter a place that reeked of puke. I had just regained my composure by five, heard my mum shouting by six, and was now sloppily mopping the floorboards at seven. Thankfully, she hadn't smelt me yet because I hadn't even physically set my eyes on her this morning; I only heard her singing praise songs miles away from my room door, so I got away with this stench.

The floor looked more slimy than clean, and the little specs of dirt hiding in each soap bubble let me know that Diana truly didn't sweep the grounds that she was assigned to sweep. She had just waved the broom around like a witch casting a spell, then flung the broom at the back of the store before disappearing into whatever fantasy land her room blessed her with. I didn't worry too much about the dirty floor anyway. Even I wasn't mopping it properly, which probably made it hazardous.

I proceeded to drag my mop around the dining table, creating a soapy ring that resembled… whatever a soapy ring resembled. After playing around with the mop for a while, I glanced at the clock and noticed it was almost 8:00 a.m. Usually I would've finished my work properly, but I had been moping this dining room for the past hour, and there was clearly no progress, perhaps except for the crocs I was wearing.

"Amanda o! Have you finished cleaning?"

"Yes ma!" Wow, this mop carried a lot of weight. Just trying to place it back in the bucket was a challenge in itself. There should be a sport for this, titled 'Mop Carrying', and the participants would be called 'Mop Carriers.'

I wheeled the bucket outside and dumped the excess water down the drainage, then left the bucket outside and carried my soaked feet back into the house. I instantly faced my mother's fuming face as she aggressively gestured towards the dining floor.

"What kind of cleaning did you just do?! You call this cleaning?!"

She then dived into a huge rant about how she used to mop both the floors and the ceilings when she was growing up: how she would tightly squeeze out the excess water from the mop, how she would climb a ladder because she was so short that even the long mop couldn't touch the ceiling, how she would use one arm to mop the kitchen floors and the other arm to flip akara. She narrated all of it to me. Countless times.

I was exhausted and had tuned out of her TedTalk (more like African nag) and was trying to think about other important things, such as the I.O.R., Cynthia's troubled sister, my dad's feud with Mr. Aloba, and who was it that entered my room during the night. They weren't blissful thoughts, but they were better than the usual reflections.

"Madam, you will come and clean this place again. What kind of nonsense is this now?!" She hissed loudly before returning to the kitchen. My dad then appeared in the dining area, didn't so much as take a look at the floor my mum was complaining about as he went into the kitchen to talk to her. I tiptoed towards it, hoping to make out what he was saying.

"That insolent man." I heard him growl as the sounds of plates clanking together hit my ears.

"Honey, you've already reported him. The police are going to arrest him today, so don't worry yourself and go and eat." My mum said comfortingly.

"Wait... arrest?! Arrest who?"

"Mr. Aloba?!"

"He killed my best friend!"

I froze at this revelation.

"I know, and I can feel the pain. I was not close to him, but I feel the pain because I knew him a little."

"I should've killed him that day in the office!" My dad ranted on, ignoring my mother's comment. "Ah, if I knew earlier that he worked at my children's school."

"Shebi he's now fired from their school, and you've told the police people."

I heard him furiously switch to Bini before reverting to English.

"I will ensure that I not only sue him but that he stays in that prison for the rest of his life. I mean, can you imagine?! Tunde Fashola is gone because of him."

"You're going to the station after this, right? Ehen, you will sort that out there. Just eat fast so you can go quickly."   It wasn't lost on me that my mum was gentle with him, a trait she didn't extend to us children.

As they both switched back to their native language, I crouched back to the dining room, trying to piece together the mystery I just accidentally solved.

Wait o! That means that day in class …

Flashback

"Excuse me, sir, but did you murder someone to get this skeleton?" Bola asked with fake concern. The class erupted in harmonious laughter as Mr. Aloba adjusted his tie nervously.

"No, I did not kill anyone. This is a preserved human skull that I bought some months ago."

"Sure, you 'bought' it." Everyone continued to laugh until Mr. Aloba banged the table with his palm in annoyance. He seemed agitated, uncomposed, and shaken up. It was weird that such a flimsy joke could unnerve a teacher that much.

Present Day

So, it wasn't a joke. It wasn't a joke!

He actually did kill someone, and that someone happened to be my dad's best friend.

And now, he's been fired as my biology teacher.

"Amanda!" I snapped out of my train of thoughts and scurried into the kitchen with the mop bucket, tensing as my dad eyed me from head to toe. It was even harder to keep a straight face now that I could perceive one of the most nauseating smells in the world. Food.

He didn't wait to hear an answer before he said, "Go and clean my car, both the inside and outside of it, because I'm going out soon."

"Okay daddy." I collected his car keys from him and

headed outside. At least now I know the horrible relationship between my father and my teacher and can focus on other cases. Right?

Wrong. The story seemed much deeper than the fact that he murdered someone. There must've been a reason for it—a secret motive or something that probably forced him to commit murder. I don't even know the full details of the murder, or what weapon he used to attack his friend, or how it ended up being—as my mum said—accidental.

The heat from the sun began striking me harder as I aimlessly stood there thinking over the conversation and the possible loopholes in the mystery. Mr. Aloba didn't come across as the type of person who just, well, murdered someone!

"Amanda, better clean that car fast!" I wondered how quickly one could clean an entire car in the few minutes I'd been here. I sighed deeply and unlocked the car to dust the insides first, but my eyes fell on a familiar tool I had forgotten about. I dug my hand deep into the corner and fished out the item that caught my attention when he was taking us to school on Wednesday. It was surprisingly in a huge Ziploc bag that had been twisted multiple times, but the item was still clearly visible.

"What could this be?" I asked myself. I unwrapped the Ziploc to get a better look at the item and noticed it was a screwdriver with a bent tip that was covered in dried blood stains. I tried to imagine what it could've possibly been used for, but a deep male voice silenced my questions and yanked the item out of my hands.

"I told you to clean my car, not touch my things! "My first thought was, "Well, that's unreasonable considering I have to move things around to clean the car."

But then, did he just say that the bent-tip, bloody screwdriver belonged to him? How?! Why would such an item be in his car in the first place?

He impatiently shooed me away from his car, which I hadn't cleaned at all, and slammed the door shut as I stared in confusion. I had so many questions that I couldn't even properly piece them together, yet all I could do was silently watch him reverse and slowly disappear from my sight while I stupidly clutched onto the dirty rag I was supposed to clean with.

I could hear my mum calling me back inside, but I continued standing underneath the scorching sun, gazing in the direction my dad had zoomed into. I just couldn't stop staring; it was as if I was hypnotized and ordered to stand in that spot, dazed and in need of direction.

My mum's shouts were getting louder by the second, but my mind wanted to create a reasonable excuse for the bloody weapon that slept soundly in my dad's car.
He couldn't have attacked anyone with it. It was probably just paint or red dye.

Or maybe he's secretly acting now, and that's a

generationally passed prop.

"I have been calling you since, and yet you acted as if you were deaf and dumb!" By now, my mum had emerged from the house with a broom in her hand. I pulled myself away from the theatre of my mind because I knew the broom wasn't for sweeping.

"You've not finished cleaning the dining room yet; you're standing like a statue. Better enter inside now and go and wash that rag!" She stood firmly at the entrance to see how I'd buzz in without getting whipped by the broom.

"I'm sorry, mummy."

"Sorry for yourself." She impatiently started gesturing for me to get inside, and all I could do was quickly look back towards the gate, sigh, and successfully enter the house without earning new broom marks on my skin. I then quickly grabbed the mop and resumed my daily chores while my mum shouted at me a little more before retiring to the kitchen. The clanking of pots merged with the sound of the running tap, meaning she was slowly disengaging from her reality and was pouring out the rest of her emotions into the meal she was preparing, which meant the food would have an additional ingredient in it today: anger.

After disconnecting from the sounds coming from the kitchen, I felt light buzzes in my right pocket, but knowing that if I brought out my phone and spoke on the phone, it would also summon my mother. I ignored the relaxing vibration and continued flinging the mop around in an attempt to clean the floors again. With the way the floor was slowly turning into a bubble bath instead of a polished marble, I knew there was no way I would effectively finish this chore, so I put my hand underneath the water dispenser and began splashing water all over the floor until the ratio of soap to water lessened. Eventually, I covered the entire living room and wiped it back and forth with the mop. Then I dumped the leftover soapy water outside and left the bucket to dry there. I told myself that whatever I did to the mop was the equivalent of washing it, similar to how I concluded that putting my hand under running water for five seconds was the same as washing it. I dried my wet hands using my wet joggers (didn't make sense, but I did it anyway) and was finally able to reply to the buzzing sounds from almost twenty minutes ago.

"Oh right, Danielle." I mumbled while struggling to control my phone screen, whose icons were darting all over as a result of my moist fingers. Just trying to tap the icons was like struggling with demons, but thankfully, I was able to pick up once it rang again.

Danielle: Amanda, finally! I know you were supposed to let me know when you were free, but I have news!
Amanda: Oh, sorry, mum asked me to do some chores.

Danielle: *I'm not bothered by that! Apparently Mr. Aloba is no longer our biology teacher.*
Amanda: *Really?*
Danielle: *And he's getting arrested for murder!*

That's strange. It hasn't even been an hour since my dad left the—

Oh, right! He had already reported him before leaving.

But then, where did she get this info from?

Amanda: *Really?*
Danielle: *Yeah, he apparently killed someone.*
Amanda: *And how do you know all of this?*
Danielle: *The news caught the story pretty quickly. It's all over Channels TV.*

Well, that answered the question.

Amanda: *Already?*
Danielle: *Yes! And apparently the person he killed was the assistant director of WEFA Bank, the bank your dad works at.*
Amanda: *Oh, wow, that's strange.*
Danielle: *Hmmm, you knew about this already, didn't you? You don't sound shocked at all.*

God, why did you make Danielle quick-witted?

My mum's voice helped put a pause in the conversation. "Somebody should turn on the TV! Diana or Amanda, turn on the TV!" With how loud she was shouting our names, I figured that was the perfect time to cut the call with Danielle and sprinted into the living room.

"Turn on the TV o!" My mum was now out of the kitchen as well and had snatched the remote out of my palms. She began switching channels faster than I blinked, and my anxiety rose with every channel that flew by. I watched impatiently as she tirelessly searched for the right channel, not realizing that my sister had also entered the living room with the most confused expression written all over her face.

"What's going on?" The question wasn't directed at any specific person, but with my mum's full concentration on our TV, it was clear that I was the sanest person at that moment who could wipe the question marks off her face.
I slowly turned my head towards her; my answer stuck deep inside my throat. She finally made eye contact with me, and her raised left eyebrow pestered me for an answer.
"I'm not sure either." She hissed, rolled her eyes, and walked past me, stopping a few metres away from our nervous mother.

"Where is it oo… ehen!" My mother finally regained her composure and proceeded to max out the volume on the TV.

Female reporter: "—*AND HE WAS BRUTALLY MURDERED BY MR. WILLIAMS ALOBA—A BIOLOGY SCHOOL TEACHER AT THE YOUNG SCHOLARS' ACADEMY. IT WAS REPORTED THAT HE WAS KILLED WITH VICIOUS STRIKES THAT DAMAGED HIS SKULL AND HE WAS DEAD BEFORE HELP GOT TO THE SCENE. MR. ALOBA HAD FLED THE SCENE MOMENTS BEFORE HE WAS FOUND DEAD OUTSIDE OF HIS HOUSE BY HIS NEIGHBOUR, BUT SECURITY CAMERAS HAD ALREADY CAPTURED HIS FACE. HE WAS AGAIN REPORTED BY THE VICTIM'S BEST FRIEND AND COLLEAGUE, MR. RICHARD EKHATOR, THE DIRECTOR OF WEFA BANK.*"

"Thank God! They've arrested him!" My mother began to rejoice and rattle off Bible verses, while I just stared at the screen in pure disbelief. I felt—no, I knew there was something strange about that entire story, but I couldn't pinpoint what it was. And to top it all off, my father appeared on screen and was talking about the case with unbridled rage. Now, our family was going to experience a great deal of unwanted attention.

As all these thoughts tangled with one another in my mind, my sister yawned listlessly and mumbled words that snapped me out of my trance.

"Well, at least one of them is dead now."

The Masquerade Ball
Anita Obehi-Ayemhere